## *"Good. Let's shake on it."*

Nick thrust his hand out at Callie, but she was wise now to what taking his hand would do to her. She shoved her hands into her jean pockets and took a step back. "No, that's okay. We have a deal."

Nick stood up. "I make it a point to seal any deals I make," he said, advancing on her.

"We . . . we don't need to," she stammered, backing even further away.

"Oh, yes we do," he said, and took a step closer to her. "But I've noticed that you don't like shaking hands. Perhaps something a little more genteel would suit you better."

She didn't think she liked the all-too-familiar glint she saw in his eyes. She stepped back again and ran up against the edge of a solidly built oak bookcase. "What did you have in mind?"

"I thought you'd never ask." And before she had a chance to react, he leaned over and brushed a kiss across her lips. "Do we have a deal?" he asked, eyes now softening to a tender blue.

Callie could only nod. For if she'd thought she'd felt some sort of current between them before, it was nothing compared to the sensations she was experiencing now. When his mouth had touched hers, he had set her on fire. And she knew, deep within her, the flames would never be put out.

Dear Reader,

Happy Spring! It's May, the flowers are blooming and love is in the air. It's the month for romance—both discovery and renewal—the month for mothers and the time of new birth. It's a wonderful time of year!

And in this special month, we have some treats in store for you. Silhouette Romance's DIAMOND JUBILEE is in full swing, and *Second Time Lucky* by Victoria Glenn is bound to help you get into the springtime spirit. Lovely heroine Lara discovers that sometimes love comes from unexpected sources when she meets up with handsome, enigmatic Miles. Don't miss this tender tale! Then, in June, *Cimarron Knight*, the first book in Pepper Adams's exciting new trilogy— *CIMARRON STORIES*—will be available. Set on the plains of Oklahoma, these three books are a true delight.

The DIAMOND JUBILEE—Silhouette Romance's tenth anniversary celebration—is our way of saying thanks to you, our readers. To symbolize the timelessness of love, as well as the modern gift of the tenth anniversary, we're presenting readers with a DIAMOND JUBILEE Silhouette Romance title each month, penned by one of your favorite Silhouette Romance authors. In the coming months writers such as Marie Ferrarella, Lucy Gordon, Dixie Browning, Phyllis Halldorson—to name just a few—are writing DIAMOND JUBILEE titles especially for you.

And that's not all! Laurie Paige has a heartwarming duo coming up—*Homeward Bound*. The first book, *A Season for Homecoming*, is coming your way in June. Peggy Webb also has *Venus de Molly*, a sequel to *Harvey's Missing*, due out in July. And much-loved Diana Palmer has some special treats in store during the months ahead....

I hope you'll enjoy this book and all of the stories to come. Come home to romance—Silhouette Romance—for always!

Sincerely,
Tara Hughes Gavin
Senior Editor

# SUSAN KALMES

# Sassafras Street

*Silhouette* *Romance*

Published by Silhouette Books New York

**America's Publisher of Contemporary Romance**

To my father,
who told me stories and let me dream

SILHOUETTE BOOKS
300 E. 42nd St., New York, N.Y. 10017

ISBN: 0-373-08721-7

First Silhouette Books printing May 1990

**Books by Susan Kalmes**

Silhouette Romance

*The Sweetheart Waltz* #564
*Sassafras Street* #721

---

## SUSAN KALMES

is a former English teacher with a lifelong passion for words. "When I was little, I used to pick a word for the week and practice saying it until it drove my mother crazy." Susan met her husband, Steve, on a blind date, became engaged to him the next day and has been a believer in love at first sight ever since. They live in Alaska and, with their two small children, spend as much time as they can camping, fishing and traveling around the "Last Frontier."

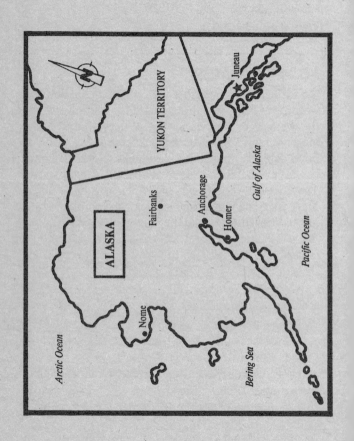

# Chapter One

The sky was bluer than she'd ever seen it. But Callie shivered inside her coat, chilled in spite of the bright sunshine. After all, she told herself, it was still only March in Anchorage, hardly spring yet.

"What do I hear for this solid oak nightstand," the auctioneer intoned, and Callie shifted her gaze back to the makeshift podium.

"Solid oak veneer," she muttered under her breath.

"It's still a nice piece."

Callie hadn't realized she'd spoken loud enough to be overheard. She turned to look at the man next to her, noticing him for the first time. Even though she didn't know his name, she recognized him. For the past six months or so he'd shown up at only the most promising auctions around town, and with shrewd bids and lots of money, always going for—and usually getting—the best antiques. That combined with his tall, broad-shouldered good looks and intensely blue eyes made him hard to forget.

"You bidding?" she asked, eyes narrowed speculatively. She'd bid against him more than once and lost out to him more times than she cared to remember.

He smiled. "I said it was a nice piece, not a great one."

She suddenly didn't like his cocky self-assurance. "And you only buy great pieces?"

His smile widened. "I like to think so."

What a shame, she thought briefly, that such good looks had to be spoiled by such a towering ego.

"Sold," the auctioneer whooped, banging a large gavel on the lectern and pointing to a triumphant auction-goer.

Callie pulled her attention away from the dark-haired man at her side and turned back to the business at hand. She was only bidding on one piece and it was next. As the auctioneer lifted the small, blackened bit of jewelry up for the crowd's inspection, Callie caught her breath. It was such a pretty piece, sterling silver with a large peridot, most definitely Edwardian and worth much, much more than it looked.

"Who will start the bidding with twenty-five dollars?"

Callie almost laughed at the ridiculously low opening bid. At this rate she would get the small pendant for almost nothing. "Twenty-five," she called, raising her numbered sign.

"Twenty-five it is to number fourteen. Do I hear thirty?"

The man at Callie's side raised his number. "Thirty to number fifty-six. Do I hear forty?" the auctioneer chanted.

Callie chanced a look at the man beside her and found his eyes resting expectantly on her. "Forty," she said, responding to the challenge so apparent in his face.

The auctioneer sensed an impending bidding war and his eyes lit up. "Fifty to you, sir."

The man gave her a conspiratorial wink. "Let's make this interesting, shall we? Two hundred dollars."

The crowd stirred, and Callie had to fight an urge to glare at her opponent. Of all the crazy things to do, she fumed, jump the bid up like that. He ought to know better. It would in all probability fuel a bidding war from some third or even fourth party and put the pendant out of her reach. "Two ten," she ground out to the waiting auctioneer.

"Don't be so fainthearted," the stranger chided, laughter in his low voice. "It takes the fun out of it."

"I'm not here for fun," Callie shot back, provoked by his frivolous attitude. "I'm here to buy antiques."

"Sir, your bid," the auctioneer called.

The man raised his number, waved it nonchalantly and said, "Three hundred."

Callie felt her quick temper explode. "Of all the stupid moves," she snapped. "The bidding would still be below a hundred if you hadn't started this incomprehensible game."

"But if I'm right, the value of the pendant approaches fifteen hundred dollars." There was still a hint of laughter in his voice, but now it also held an uncompromising certainty.

Surprised, Callie turned to study him once again. For all the smooth blandness in the look he gave her, she saw a glint of keen intelligence in his eye. So, he knew antique jewelry. Well, he didn't know it as well as she did. She was one of the sharpest dealers in the area. Everyone in the business knew it and respected her for it. She'd beat this guy at his own game. "Think what you like," she shrugged, hoping to rattle his self-confidence with a little reverse psychology. "It's a good copy, that's all."

"Then why are you so interested in it?"

"Sentimental value," she responded quickly. "An aunt of mine used to have one like it." And that aunt, Jessie by name, had impulsively given it away and now regretted her action.

"Your bid," the man reminded her, and Callie quickly raised her number, nodding at the auctioneer. "Three ten."

The man with the blue eyes didn't even blink. "Four hundred."

Callie knew she should pull out. She'd given herself a four-hundred-dollar limit and she made it a practice never to go over her self-imposed cutoff point. But this man with his knowing eyes and too-confident smile needed to be taught a lesson—taken down a peg or two—and she was just the person to do it. "Five hundred," she said smoothly and felt a rush of satisfaction.

"Six," and the man at her side tossed her an approving smile.

"Seven," she responded and then blanched when he raised the bid to a thousand. This was getting into serious money, money she would have to account for to another of her aunts, Maude. But Caledonia Baker rarely shrank from a challenge. "Eleven hundred," she called, and the crowd began to murmur with excitement.

"Twelve," her adversary said, and Callie responded immediately.

"Thirteen."

"Fifteen."

This is insanity, she told herself, the shock of just how high the bid had gotten cooling her ardor somewhat. The pendant wasn't worth any more than fifteen hundred dollars and then, only if some collector wanted to pay that much. As a dealer she was supposed to buy low and sell high, not risk her money, or rather her aunt's money on a whim. But she just couldn't back down now. "Sixteen," she finally called, although she had to do it through suddenly chattering teeth.

There was only silence from the blue-eyed man next to her, and she thought she'd won. But at what a price! She was already searching for a plausible explanation to give to her Aunt Maude when he upped the bid again.

"Two thousand."

Callie shook her head at the auctioneer and after no more bids were forthcoming, he rapped his gavel and pronounced the bidding over. Callie turned to her rival, relief warring with defeat. "You could have had it for three hundred less," she said, a sort of grim satisfaction in her voice, and without another word turned to go.

He caught hold of her arm. "Would you like to join me for a cup of coffee somewhere?" He gave her that confident grin. "We could console each other."

She looked at his hand for a moment. It seemed so proprietorial somehow, as if he'd staked a claim not only on the pendant but on her, as well. The thought disturbed and intrigued her at the same time. "Why should you be consoled?" she finally asked, her voice sounding far off even to her own ears. "You won."

"I just paid double what I should have for that pendant. I hardly call that winning."

She looked up at him and had the most curious sensation of falling into the twin pools of his eyes. "Then why did you do it?"

He shrugged and let his hand fall away. "I never back down from a fight."

"Bloodied but unbowed?"

"Something like that."

Callie shivered, suddenly glad she wouldn't have to go head-to-head with him again. She, too, liked to win and wasn't sure she ever would with a man like this as her opponent.

"So, how about that cup of coffee?" he reminded her.

"No, thanks. I have to get back to work."

"Surely the boss wouldn't mind if you took an extra half hour break."

"I'm my own boss," she said shortly. "Now, if you'll excuse me..." Without waiting for the reply she knew was coming, she stepped past him and hurried away.

She tried to put him from her mind as she maneuvered her car through the snow-laden streets of Anchorage. But in spite of her good intentions, she found herself reliving every moment of their bidding war, wondering why he had started it in the first place and what might have happened if she'd agreed to join him for a cup of coffee. She thought about the way his hand had felt on her arm and shivered again. "Forget about him, Caledonia," she told herself as she pulled her car into her usual parking spot. "You've got other things to worry about."

But as she hurried up Sassafras Street toward Baker's Antiques and Collectibles, she managed to forget her problems for the time being. The day was just too beautiful to be ignored. The wind was blowing out of the south, whistling through the mountains, bringing with it the smell of the sea and the subtle feel of spring. Callie realized the change of seasons was still weeks if not months away; but spring was in her bones and she knew from many years of experience that it wouldn't be long before it spread its magic over the cold, frozen land.

She breezed into Baker's Antiques and Collectibles, rattling the door shut behind her. "Aunt Jessie," she called. "Where are you?"

"No need to shout, Callie. I'm right here."

Callie shed her bright red coat and gloves and stamped the snow from her boots. The interior of Baker's was dim and full of shadows after the brilliant sunshine outside. Even allowing for the time it took her eyes to adjust, Callie had to admit it was always dim and shadowy in Baker's. But that was half its charm. "Where, Aunt Jessie? I still can't see a thing."

"I'm in the armoire."

Callie smiled. Now why didn't that surprise her? "Why are you in the armoire, Aunt Jessie?"

The answer was muffled. "Shadow's having her kittens today and I'm assisting."

Callie hung her coat on a tarnished brass hall tree and smoothed her hair. "Anything I can do?"

"Just mind the store, my dear. I may be a while."

Shadow, their calico cat, was a splendid if infrequent mother. Aunt Jessie had assisted at every delivery, never losing her wonder at the miracle of new life. The bedside scenes took place in the most unusual places, however, causing Aunt Jessie to spend a great deal of time in packing crates, clawfooted bathtubs, cobweb-covered corners and now a massive oak armoire.

"I didn't get the necklace," Callie called. "I had to battle some man for it, and he outbid me. It made me angry." *He* made her angry would have been more apt.

"That's nice, dear."

Callie realized that Aunt Jessie wasn't listening. Oh, well, there wasn't much else to say, really.

Callie threaded her way through mounds of old furniture and miscellaneous bric-a-brac to the rear of the shop where her costume for the day awaited her. She and Aunt Jessie had decided she should wear some of their vintage clothing around the store. "It adds to the atmosphere," Aunt Jessie had insisted over Callie's initial protests.

"But what if I ruin something?" Callie had objected.

"Why, we'll just write it off as a business expense," had come her great-aunt's blithe reply.

That was Aunt Jessie's problem, Callie thought now as she stepped behind a nineteenth-century changing screen and tugged off her blue jeans. She had no business sense. None whatsoever. She gave away as much as she ever sold, always a soft touch for someone down on his luck or in love with something he couldn't afford. And that's what had landed them in their present predicament.

Baker's Antiques and Collectibles had hovered on the brink of bankruptcy for years, never quite going under but never showing a profit, either. It didn't seem to bother Aunt Jessie, but it kept her in constant hot water with her sister and not-so-silent business partner, Maude.

Callie shed her sweatshirt and stepped into a ruffled petticoat. Aunt Maude, now there was a tough customer. Where Jessie was petite, Maude was massive. Jessie had a cloud of white hair, Maude a helmet of careful curls the color of a battleship. Where Jessie lacked business sense, that was all Maude was. And she had finally pulled the plug on Baker's. "I'll not pour another dime down that rat hole until things change," she'd barked long distance from her home in California after she'd received their last financial statement. "As of now, I'm assuming control of the business."

Callie tugged on a pair of old-fashioned, high-top shoes with sixty little buttons. She knew; she'd counted them yesterday. "Can't I wear my own boots?" she'd questioned Aunt Jessie. The answer had been a kind, but very firm no. Now, as she wielded a long-handled buttonhook, Callie had time to ponder the ramifications of the pronouncement that Maude was taking control of Baker's.

At first there had been little change, just no more ready cash to help them meet any additional expenses other than the fixed monthly ones. That's why her bidding war had been such a descent into lunacy. To come up with an extra fifteen hundred dollars at this point would have been close to impossible.

And then to top off what had become an almost intolerable situation, Maude had written her that she had hired a new manager for the store. Callie was still outraged at the arbitrary decision. If she had ever been given a chance to manage the store on her own terms without interference from either of her great-aunts, it would be a going concern now. She'd tried to make the point to Aunt Maude but her arguments had been summarily dismissed. "I've made up my mind, Caledonia, and that's final. Nicholas Logan has been hired to turn that business around. Now, you either make up your mind to help him or find a new job." Aunt Maude was big on minds being made up.

Callie had followed Aunt Maude's advice and, grudgingly to be sure, decided to help him. She didn't want another job. She loved Baker's and all of their customers. She knew she wouldn't be happy anyplace else. And surely, once this Nicholas Logan recognized her abilities, he would at the very least share the running of the store with her. Perhaps even realize he was redundant and look for some other store to run, leaving Baker's to her.

With this rosy picture in mind, Callie fastened the last of the tiny shoe buttons and turned to her dress. It was beautiful, she admitted as she slipped it from its padded hanger. The color of warm taffy, the gown was in the Victorian style with full, leg-o-mutton sleeves, a ruffled silk Venice lace collar and a long, billowing skirt that swept to a small train in the back. Totally impractical for anything even closely resembling work. But still beautiful.

By the time Callie had the sixty-four hooks and eyes fastened up the back of the dress, her arms felt like they were going to break. But the exercise had given her a few more minutes to think. According to Maude, this Nicholas Logan had been due in town yesterday.

As anxious as Callie was to look him over, she was just that anxious to postpone the inevitable for as long as possible. She was sure he would be old, full of himself and his knowledge of antiques and probably every bit as crotchety as Aunt Maude.

"I'll just fix him a hot toddy now and again. That should keep him happy," she murmured, and then laughed at the scenario playing in her head. She could see him now, a white-haired old man, sour faced from a solitary life lived out amongst other people's antiques, softening under the influence of her liberally spiked hot toddies, eventually asking her, no, begging her to take over the running of the store.

Callie shrugged away the pleasant scene and ran a brush through her long hair, parting it across her head and combing the front half down over her eyes while she quickly braided and rolled the back half. No use dreaming about the impossible.

She was twisting the heavy mass of hair on top of her head when the front door opened. "Be with you in a minute," she called through a mouthful of tortoiseshell hairpins.

"Excuse me," a chillingly familiar voice interrupted not a moment later.

Startled, Callie jumped and felt her precarious hairdo begin to slide. She'd know that deep voice anywhere. It belonged to the man from the auction this morning. Probably here to offer her an opportunity to buy the necklace, she thought grimly. Well, she wouldn't, not even if he cut a thousand dollars off the price. "If you could just give me a minute," she said coldly, unable to see through the curtain of hair still hanging over her eyes.

"You're Miss Baker, I presume," he went on as if she hadn't spoken.

"I am," she said even as she wondered how he'd found out her name. Of course it wasn't as if she were unknown in the antique-hunting crowd at the auction. He could have asked almost anyone there and they would have supplied him with the information.

"But not Miss Jessica Baker." There was a hint of amusement in his voice now.

What could he possibly want with Aunt Jessie? And then she felt her quick temper begin to stir. Maybe he thought he could con her aunt into buying the necklace at some outrageously inflated amount. "My name," she said with steely emphasis as she jabbed hairpins into her teetering coiffure, "is Caledonia Baker and if you think—" but he interrupted her.

"Ah, yes, Caledonia," he said as if he knew her. "Interesting name."

Finally she had the last pin in place and the hair out of her face. "And you are . . . ?" she asked, having to steady herself at the slight trembling that began in her knees when she turned and saw those blue eyes again.

"Nicholas Logan. Nick—" he paused to give her a slight smile "—to my friends."

She was literally robbed of breath. This was Nicholas Logan, white-haired, sour-faced Nicholas Logan? It just couldn't be, and she shook her head in confused denial. Her life, which had seemed so complicated only moments before, now took on the aspect of a Chinese puzzle.

At her hesitation, he turned coolly businesslike. "I believe I'm expected."

"No...I mean, yes," she blurted out. This far-too-handsome man was totally unexpected, but she wasn't going to tell him that. "But you're supposed to be from California."

"I am," he said calmly.

"But I've seen you around town at different auctions off and on for the last six months or so. I've even bid against you myself." And then she grew suspicious. Was he some sort of spy for Aunt Maude? Had he been following her to anonymously test her mettle? Is that why he'd run the bid up so ridiculously high this morning, to see if she was spending Maude's money foolishly?

She gave herself a mental shake. You're getting hysterical, Callie, she chided. Of course Maude wasn't having her followed. That only happened in the movies. Didn't it?

"Perhaps it would be best if I met with Miss Jessica Baker at this time." If he was aware of her suspicious train of thought, he gave no indication of it in his impassive features.

Callie took a deep, steadying breath, determined to match his calm manner. "I'm sorry, but Miss Baker is unavailable right now."

"Callie, dear, could I bother you for a cup of tea? It looks like I might be here awhile."

Aunt Jessie's timing couldn't have been worse. "Just a minute, Aunt Jessie," Callie called, withstanding a wild desire to run and hide from the relentless gaze of Nick Logan.

"Unavailable, you said?" he asked, one eyebrow quirked expectantly.

She felt whatever slim hope she'd had of gaining the advantage over the situation slip farther from reach. "Aunt Jessie is in the armoire," she began, and then bit her lip. This was not going to be easy.

"And," Nick prompted her, a smile tugging at the corners of his mouth.

In spite of her discomfort, she couldn't help but smile back. "You see, Shadow is having her kittens today."

Nick shook his head. "You've lost me."

Callie tried again, but for some strange reason her brain seemed to be malfunctioning. Maybe it was the half smile still playing at the corners of his mouth that upset her self-possession and made her pulse beat faster than it should. "Shadow is in the armoire and Aunt Jessie is in there with her lending moral support."

"Ah," Nick said wisely. "And would it be all right if I spoke to Miss Baker during this, uh, delicate moment?"

Suddenly Callie didn't dislike him as intensely as she had only a moment before. "Come with me." She turned and picked her way through the store toward Aunt Jessie's hiding place. Callie was aware of his eyes on her as he kept pace behind her, and once again her pulse leaped disconcertingly in her throat.

She stopped in front of the huge armoire and looked back at Nick. He was even more handsome than she had originally thought, with midnight-dark hair and eyes as blue as a forget-me-not. Too bad, she decided, that he wasn't the white-haired old man she'd imagined. He would have been easier to ignore.

"Aunt Jessie," she called.

"Yes, my dear?"

"Mr. Logan is here."

There came an agitated rustling. "Oh, dear." Aunt Jessie popped her head out of the armoire and observed them with worried, china-blue eyes. "Hello," she murmured. "My sister told us you were coming, but not exactly when. You're not anything like I'd expected. Much younger and much more handsome."

Leave it to Aunt Jessie to sum it all up in a few blunt words, Callie thought, torn between embarrassment and amusement. She risked a quick glance at Nick and was surprised to see a hint of red crawl up his neck. Well, at least he's human, she decided. She helped her great-aunt out of the armoire, aware that the frail old hand in hers trembled slightly, and any softening in her feelings toward Nick Logan evaporated. His presence in the store was going to be unendurable.

Aunt Jessie brushed the wrinkles from her skirt and patted her hair into place. "Shadow has had four kittens so far," she said with a slightly wavering smile in

Nick's direction. "You will let them stay in the store, won't you?"

Callie didn't know whether to cry or turn to Nick Logan and scream at him like a fishwife. This had been Aunt Jessie's store longer than forever. It wasn't right that she had to ask a perfect stranger for permission.

Nick put out a hand to Aunt Jessie and touched her lightly on the arm, his gesture one of comfort. "Of course they can stay, Miss Baker."

"Call me Aunt Jessie," she said, relief apparent in her suddenly happy voice. "Everyone does." She turned to Callie and patted her on the cheek. "There, you see? Nothing to worry about. Now, I really must return to Shadow. Caledonia, please show Mr. Logan where to hang his coat. And I trust you'll also show him every kindness." Before Callie could protest, Aunt Jessie climbed back into the armoire and shut the door firmly behind her.

Silence reigned. Callie longed to follow Aunt Jessie into the armoire and get away from Nick but she knew she was trapped into staying where she was.

"Take a deep breath," he advised her with a grin.

"How do you know I need one?"

He laughed out loud. "Aside from the fact that you should never play high-stakes poker?"

"Transparent?"

"As clear glass."

"If that's true, why did you bother to bid against me this morning? You must have known when I passed my limit."

"Oh, I did. It was at about four hundred. But I also knew you wouldn't be able to resist a challenge."

"How could you know that?" she demanded.

"I recognized all the symptoms. I have the same problem."

"We'll never be able to sell the necklace here," she stated, a sort of grim satisfaction in her voice. "You threw Maude's money away."

"The necklace isn't for sale."

"But you have a great deal of Maude's money tied up in it. How are you going to explain that to her?"

"I used my own money."

"Do you collect antique jewelry?" It was a natural question. Most people in the antique business had a passion for something, be it jewelry, books, dolls or any number of other things.

His eyes rested expectantly on her face. "Let's just say, Miss Baker," he murmured, "that I wanted that necklace for a personal reason."

"Oh," she said, and wondered as she tore her eyes away from his and turned to stare out the window if that "personal" reason was someone waiting for him back in California. What difference should it make to you, she chided herself. None, she answered staunchly and once more called up all her resentment over the situation into which she'd been so unwillingly thrust. She hated Nick Logan, hated knowing that he didn't really deserve it, but hated most of all what he was already doing to upset the uneventful tenor of their lives. She wanted him gone. "Mr. Logan," she said, anger and resentment stiffening her body, "do you have any idea how high-handed all of this is?"

"No. Why don't you enlighten me?"

She turned and saw that he had crossed his arms over his chest and was leaning casually against the edge of the armoire, waiting for her tirade. Well, she wasn't going to disappoint him. "Mr. Logan, my aunt is approaching eighty. She lives frugally above this shop, wears clothes she's had for twenty years and eats practically nothing. She has two vices. This store and her pet cat, Shadow."

"I'm here to save the store for her," he said with maddening self-composure when Callie paused to take a breath.

"But don't you see? She doesn't want the store to be *saved*. That it limps along, barely making it each month, means nothing to her. She's content the way things are."

"What about you?"

Callie faltered. To say she wasn't content would seem disloyal to Aunt Jessie. But how many times had she yearned for exactly the same authority Nick Logan had been given to breathe new life into the store? It just wasn't fair that he'd gotten the opportunity that should have been hers. "The store belongs to Aunt Jessie," she told him, "not me."

"Fifty-one percent of it belongs to her sister, Maude," Nick reminded her.

"And money talks," Callie flared.

"Sometimes," he agreed.

"Life is to be lived, not counted and compounded daily."

"That's beside the point—"

"That is the point," she interrupted hotly.

Much to Callie's frustration, Nick remained calm. She was spoiling for a good, old-fashioned fight. "The point, Miss Baker, is that your Aunt Maude holds the purse strings. If she chooses to place a new manager in this store, she has the legal right to do so."

"It's not fair," Callie said, at last giving voice to her thoughts. What her pride wouldn't let her add was that by all rights, the new manager should have been her.

The smile was back, tugging at the corners of his mouth. "No, probably not."

"Caledonia," Aunt Jessie's voice echoed hollowly from the depths of the armoire. "I really must insist that you and Mr. Logan move your conversation to another part of the store. Perhaps back to our desk. You are upsetting Shadow."

Color flooded Callie's cheeks. "Please follow me," she commanded, knowing she had little choice in the matter. Careful to lift her skirts off the floor, she marched away, never looking back to see if he followed. She led him to the store's only desk, an old oak rolltop full of overflowing pigeonholes and hidden drawers. "Here are our records," she said, waving a hand over the confusion.

Nick's face held it's first hint of dismay. "This is going to be quite a . . . challenge."

For the first time in a long time, Callie actually looked past the desk to the utter chaos on top of it.

"Neither one of us likes book work very much," she confessed, realizing how bad it must look to him.

"Yes, I can see that."

"But I'm sure everything you'll need is here somewhere. This old desk is loaded with little drawers and secret nooks. If you can't find something, just keep looking."

"Can I count on your help?" he asked softly,.

It seemed too much to ask. Hot, angry words trembled on her lips, but before they could spill out, she lifted her eyes to his. She could find no malice there. Determination, yes. But understanding and, surprisingly, even some sympathy. "I suppose so," she finally agreed, although the words felt like they might choke her.

"Good. I'll need it, I'm sure." And then he turned away from her, shrugged out of his coat and seated himself in the old swivel office chair, his attention riveted on their accounts in a matter of seconds.

# Chapter Two

"Callie? Callie, dear? Come and see the kittens."

Aunt Jessie's wavering call brought Callie's attention back to the present. For the past few hours she'd existed in some sort of fog, listlessly roaming the store, unsure of what to do with herself. Her usual routine no longer seemed appropriate, at least she didn't think it did. But so far Nick had not given her any indication as to what role he wanted her to play in the running of the store.

Almost against her will, she found her gaze drawn to his dark head bent so diligently over the books. As if he felt her eyes on him, he lifted his head and looked over at her. "Do you need something?"

Chagrined that he'd caught her staring, she blurted

out the first thing to pop into her head. "Aunt Jessie wants us to see the kittens."

When first a look of surprise and then a warm smile spread over his face, Callie had more than a twinge of conscience. He must be feeling as awkward and out of place as she was. And to be honest, she hadn't been very helpful in making him feel more at ease. Innately courteous, she vowed to do better.

He got up from the desk and made his way over to her. For a moment they looked at each other, measuring, judging. And then Nick gave her that blinding smile of his. "I'll take any break from paperwork I can get. Shall we?" he said, and he ushered her toward the armoire.

"I would have thought paperwork was your strong suit," Callie said over her shoulder.

"What gives you that idea?"

They stopped in front of the armoire and she tried to explain. "I thought that's why Aunt Maude hired you, to give us a hand with the paperwork."

"Callie," he said, voice cool and once more all business, "I was hired to run this store, not just do your book work. I'm in charge, and if you work here, you work for me."

She'd been wrong about him. He wasn't feeling out of place at all. He'd stormed Baker's like a general in charge of an invading army and now expected her to give up her place to him with a handshake and a smile. Well, she had news for him. Circumstances may have forced her to retreat but she wasn't vanquished just yet.

Nick watched with interest as the tangle of emotions played out over her face. "Do we have an understanding?" he prompted, obviously relishing the duel.

"Oh, we have an understanding all right—" she began, but before she could tell him what the understanding was, that she was not going to give in to him without a fight, the door to the armoire swung open and Aunt Jessie emerged, stiff but triumphant. "Six kittens in all," she whispered, climbing out with Callie's assistance. "Just look in. Shadow won't mind."

Knowing her temper was just about to run away with her, Callie welcomed the diversion. While she poked her head inside the large cabinet, Aunt Jessie, her eyes bright with curiosity, surveyed Nick. "Are you finding everything you need?" she asked.

"So far."

"Do you have a place to stay?"

"I've got a hotel room just a few blocks away."

Aunt Jessie let her gaze wander for a moment and then she brought it back to Nick's face. "Are you married, Mr. Logan?" she asked abruptly.

Nick laughed and ran his hand through his hair. "No, Miss Baker, I'm not."

Aunt Jessie nodded once, as if satisfied. "Neither is Callie," she remarked.

"Neither is Callie, what?" Callie asked, catching the last of this.

"Married, my dear," Aunt Jessie told her blithely. "Nor is Mr. Logan. Now isn't that a coincidence?"

Callie groaned, and face suffused with color, she had to once more resist the urge to climb into the armoire and close the door behind her. Aunt Jessie had been trying to marry her off for years, but to try it with Nick Logan was just too much. He was arrogant beyond belief, egotistical to the extreme and totally wrong for her.

"Your niece was just going to show me around the store, weren't you Callie?" Nick gave her a look that challenged her to pick the lesser of the two evils—Aunt Jessie's matchmaking or his company.

Callie knew when she'd been had. "Why don't you come with us, Aunt Jessie?" she asked with saccharine sweetness and a level stare at Nick as if to say she couldn't be outmaneuvered without her consent.

"My, my, no," Aunt Jessie declared, beaming approval at them, oblivious to the daggers flying over her head from brown eyes to blue. "You two run along and do whatever you have to do. I think I'll just go on upstairs for a few minutes." She turned to Callie. "You'll keep an eye on Shadow, won't you, dear? You know she has a tendency to move her kittens."

"I promise," Callie answered.

"Have fun." Aunt Jessie fired this parting shot and hurried away to disappear up a flight of stairs positioned at the rear of the store.

"She has an apartment on the second floor," Callie explained shortly.

"Do you live up there, too?"

Callie couldn't let go of her resentment completely, but she decided to wrestle it under control. So she'd been tricked into taking him on a guided tour of the store. She would have done it sooner or later anyway. "If you think the store is crowded, you should see Aunt Jessie's apartment. There isn't any room for me up there."

"Then where do you live?" Nick persisted.

"Up the street in a little house of my own. Now, why don't we get started," she suggested crisply, and led the way to one corner of the shop. "I suppose this is as good a place to begin as any. Most of our books are here." She ran a hand along the dusty bindings and then absently rubbed her fingers over her cheek.

"You've got a smudge," Nick told her, and before she could protest, he reached out and gently wiped it away.

Something happened to her when he touched her. Something so odd, it took her breath away. Pure sensation, hot and disturbing flowed from where his hand rested on her face to spread throughout her body, constricting her chest and weakening her knees. And she didn't like it. Not one bit. But she couldn't seem to pull away from him. The warm feelings rushing through her held her immobile. "As you can see," she murmured, eyes locked with his, "we have lots of old books."

"Is there a market for them?" he asked, his own voice suddenly husky.

"Children's books go rather well."

"Do you collect them?"

Nick's fingers still lingered on her cheek, and she was finding it increasingly difficult to think. "No, antique jewelry is my specialty."

"So that explains the fierce battle for the necklace this morning. You wanted it for yourself, not Aunt Jessie."

At the mention of the bidding war in which he'd embroiled her, Callie's senses returned. She reminded herself of what she'd thought at the time, that Nick Logan was a formidable opponent. In their present situation, she'd do well to remember that and not be taken in by a pair of blue eyes and a smile that twisted her heart. "Perhaps you're right," she said, and ducked away from his hand, breaking the spell between them.

"We sell some sheet music," she said, recovering her composure as she walked on. "Old postcards, photographs, stereoscopes and the like. And then over here we start the china, pottery and glass." She showed him the Carnival, Cranberry and Depression Glass, automatically answering his questions even as her mind raced to find the reason for his puzzling effect on her.

She already knew that much of the time she didn't like him. But she'd caught an occasional glimpse of another side of him. The side that let him deal so gently with Aunt Jessie. And when he did that, he had a charm that was hard to resist. Fortunately for her, it was rare enough that she could dismiss it as inconsequential. He was much more often the fiercely competitive, audacious opponent from the auction that morning.

"Do you dress up in old clothes every day?" Nick asked, his eyes sweeping over her as they toured the vintage clothing.

Callie was immediately on the defensive. At every turn it seemed as if the store and its contents belonged to Nick and she was the interloper. "It adds to the atmosphere," she bristled, unconsciously echoing Aunt Jessie's answer to her own earlier objections.

"I agree," he answered mildly, defusing her anger. He plucked a black satin dress spangled with cut-glass beads from the rack and studied it for moment. "Why don't you wear this tonight?"

"Tonight?" she repeated, puzzled.

"When I take you out to dinner."

The last thing on earth she wanted to do was go out with Nick Logan. "No, I couldn't possibly...."

Aunt Jessie chose that moment to make her reappearance, interrupting Callie's refusal. "Couldn't possibly what?"

There was nothing wrong with Aunt Jessie's hearing, Callie thought wryly, for all her almost eighty years. "Go out to dinner with Nick," she muttered.

"Nonsense. Of course you'll go. And wear the black satin Mr. Logan is holding. You'll look lovely in it."

"Aunt Jessie, I don't think this is a very good idea." That was an understatement to say the least. Callie knew that it would be a fatal mistake to blur the lines between business and pleasure with this man.

It was almost as if Aunt Jessie could read her mind. "You'll want to discuss business, won't you?" she asked, appealing to Nick. At his nod, she smiled happily. "See, Callie, dear, it's a business meeting."

"Then why don't *you* go out with him?" It was a reasonable argument; after all, the store belonged to Aunt Jessie, not her.

Aunt Jessie actually giggled. "That wouldn't do at all. Black is not my color. Now—" she patted Callie on the arm as if the matter were settled to everyone's complete satisfaction "—you two continue on with your tour. I'll just pop in on Shadow and check her condition."

With a feeling of defeat, Callie turned and took the dress out of Nick's hands. "What time tonight?" she asked with resignation.

She missed the amused, slightly sardonic smile that curved his mouth. "What time do we close?"

"Six."

"How about seven?"

"Fine," Callie said, crushing the black satin in her hands. "I'll be ready at seven."

Callie sat in the hushed splendor of one of Anchorage's finest rooftop restaurants, gazing out over the brilliant city lights below them. "It's beautiful here," she said, sighing, and found that her mood had mellowed with the night.

Nick sat beside her. "I'm glad you like it."

She turned to him and smiled, her eyes the color of brown sugar in the candlelight. "What's there not to like? The food was delicious, the decor is . . . is fabulous." She gestured around her at the pale apricot walls and sparkling chandeliers, the rich beige carpet and lush tropical plants. "And the view." She sighed again with utter contentment. "It's like sitting in heaven."

Nick smiled his agreement. "It is pretty spectacular, although a lot tamer than I'd imagined. I thought I'd be met at the airport by a couple of bears and a moose or two."

She feigned wide-eyed sincerity. "They were probably watching you from the woods."

"Do you think so?" he asked, and then glimpsed the laughter dancing in her eyes. "Seriously, are there any bears in the city itself?"

"Sure, but it's winter now and all the good little bears are still sound asleep."

"It's not the *good* little bears I'm worried about," he said, and she laughed at his wry humor.

She propped her chin on her hand, interested in him in spite of herself. "So tell me, Nick, what do you think of Alaska beyond your disappointment at the lack of a proper welcoming committee?"

"It's cold."

"Your blood is thin from all that California sun," she teased. "It's not cold now, just brisk."

"You call ten degrees brisk?"

Callie laughed. "Anchorage is in the banana belt of Alaska. You should go to Fairbanks if you want cold, or up to the North Slope. Ten degrees is a regular heat wave for them."

Nick shook his head. "Too cold for me. How about you, do you like it here?"

He sounded so dubious, Callie had to laugh again. She wondered briefly if she ought to lie about how she felt. After all, if she painted a bleak picture of Alaska it might help persuade him to leave. But then her natural honesty took over. "I love it here," she said. "It's the most beautiful place on earth, and I've seen lots of other places. The mountains, the ocean, the flowers in the summertime, whales in Cook Inlet, eagles on the wind, all of it takes my breath away."

She paused for a moment and then asked him what she'd had on her mind since he'd walked into Baker's that morning. "Do you plan on staying here, permanently, I mean? Or is this temporary, just until the store turns around?"

"I don't think anyone can know what their permanent plans are. Life has a way of changing when you least expect it." As he spoke, his eyes, full of some emotion she couldn't identify, came to rest on her face. "But in answer to your question, yes, I plan on staying here, at least for the foreseeable future."

She was disappointed at the news, but at the same time she felt a curious sense of exhilaration, too, and couldn't understand why.

"More wine?" he asked and at her nod, poured her another glass. "Now it's your turn, Callie," he said, encouraging her with one of his most beguiling smiles. "Tell me about yourself."

"What do you want to know?" she answered, aware that he'd turned his not inconsiderable charm on her.

She knew she should resist but couldn't seem to muster the necessary will. The night was just too seductive.

"For starters, where did the name Caledonia come from? I don't think I've ever heard of it before."

"My dad named me that," she answered. "He was a romantic at heart and when he saw my red hair for the first time, he told my mother no other name would do. Literally translated, it means 'Scotland.'"

For a moment she traveled back in time, remembering how she'd felt as a little girl, nestled on her father's lap, listening intently while he filled her head with tales of Highland chieftains and heather-laden moors, of Bonny Prince Charlie and the battle of Culloden, of the clans and the plaids and the mist-covered mountains.

In her room at night, she'd often imagined herself to be a princess in exile, a princess waiting to be carried away by one of those wild and daring Scotsmen. He would come to her with a skirl of bagpipes and sprig of heather, come to take her to his castle in the sky.

"Callie?"

She floated back to the present, unaware of the memories that still clouded her eyes, and she idly wondered as she looked over at Nick if his ancestors had once roamed the Scottish highlands. "Hmm?"

"Where did you go?"

She smiled sadly for those far distant dreams. "Back home for a minute."

"Where's that?"

"I grew up in Santa Fe, New Mexico. I came up here to live with Aunt Jessie after my folks died."

"They're both gone?"

She nodded. "Mom of a long illness. Dad afterward of a broken heart. It happened years ago."

"And you've been here ever since?"

Callie nodded. "Aunt Jessie and I have been a team for a long time. She took me in, mothered me, let me crash my way through adolescence in the store. And then when my hands and feet weren't quite so gawky anymore and I'd quit breaking things, she taught me everything I know. It's been quite a partnership." She paused for a sip of wine. "So what about you? Are you originally from California?"

"I'm a native, all right." He said it with a mixture of pride and rueful surprise, as if native Californians were an oddity.

She rested her chin on her hand again, once more overcome with curiosity. "How did you ever get interested in antiques?"

"I guess you could say I was born to it. My mother is an avid collector, so I grew up in a house full of them. And my dad owns a very successful antique business in L.A."

"Why did you decide to come up here?"

He flashed her a grin. "I got tired of surfing."

She could see that he was teasing. "No, really," she persisted. "I'd like to know. Most people wouldn't trade California for Alaska."

"Maude Baker made me an offer I couldn't refuse."

Callie couldn't imagine an offer attractive enough to entice him away from a successful family business. "Your folks must be disappointed you left."

He gave an almost bitter laugh. "My folks were happy to get rid of me."

"I don't believe that."

"Maybe that is a bit overstated. Let's just say my dad and I don't see eye to eye on everything."

If Nick and his father were anything alike, Callie thought, fireworks would be inevitable. "Then what happened?" she asked.

"I left," he said shortly.

"Did your dad kick you out or did you run away?"

"Neither one," he said, bristling.

She'd really only meant to tease him a little and his abrupt response surprised her. She wondered if there might be some truth in one or even both of her assumptions, but she didn't pursue it. "How on earth do you know Aunt Maude?"

"Through the business in California. She's been a client for years. At first she commissioned me to come up here a few times, take a look around and assess the general business climate of the area. I took the opportunity while I was here to attend some auctions and even buy some antiques for my folk's store. After I made my report to Maude, she offered me the job running Baker's. I was looking for something at the time, so I jumped at it."

That answered one of Callie's questions and brought her to the most burning one of all. "What are your plans for our store?"

He took a deep breath and while his eyes took on a certain remoteness, they never left her face. "I'm going to close it down."

"You're what? On whose authority?" Callie's voice was so sharp it caused several people sitting close to them to glance in their direction. But she didn't care about the curious murmurs her outburst had raised. She was caught in the grip of anger so profound, she thought she might explode with it.

"Calm down," he ordered, "and let me explain."

She knew suddenly that this was why he'd taken her out to dinner in the most expensive restaurant in town, so that after he'd dropped his little bombshell, she wouldn't be able to create a scene. Well, he didn't know her very well. "I won't calm down. How dare you come in here and in one day decide to close Baker's down." She got to her feet, ready to leave.

"Hear me out before you go bolting out of here."

His voice held such cold authority, she automatically sank back into her seat, hating herself for responding to the order even as she complied. "You've got exactly one minute, Mr. Logan, and then I'm leaving." She gestured to the remains of their lavish meal. "Your purchase price wasn't nearly high enough."

He had the good grace to blush, but his eyes never wavered. "Callie, I invited you here because I wanted to get to know you better. I could have said all this at Baker's and saved myself a headache."

It was Callie's turn to blush. It wasn't easy to think of herself as a headache. "Tell me about the store," she said with icy composure, proud of the control she'd regained over her emotions.

"As it stands, Baker's is an aging, rundown store that, without help, has little hope of turning around. I've been hired to give it that help. First of all the store needs a facelift. The nature and extent of that facelift will depend upon several factors."

In spite of herself, Callie felt her interest stir to life. "Which are?"

"The neighborhood for one. I need to look around, talk to some of the other store owners, identify some business trends. In other words, I need to see if Sassafras Street is economically stable. If it isn't, then I'll recommend a different course of action to your Aunt Maude."

Callie didn't have to ask what that recommendation would be. She knew Aunt Maude well enough to know she'd shut Baker's down completely if it couldn't be made to turn a profit. Callie would do everything in her power to keep that from happening, even if it meant swallowing her pride and getting along with Nick Logan. "What else?" she prompted.

"The cost of renovation. According to the figures I have, labor costs in Anchorage are prohibitive."

"There's no way around that."

"Again, it depends on how extensive a renovation we need. I can do some of the simple things myself. While I was at college, I worked construction during summer breaks."

"What will Aunt Jessie and I do?"

"You can help me." It was more an order than a request and Callie felt her resentment flash again.

"And Aunt Jessie?"

"Ah, Aunt Jessie..." he began, but then his voice trailed away and he wouldn't meet her eyes.

"What?" she asked, her heart suddenly twisting with fear. "What about Aunt Jessie?"

"Callie," he asked, "don't you think she needs more than a failing antique store, a pet cat and a bunch of dusty old books? She could use some companionship with people her own age, travel, retirement."

Callie shook her head vehemently, and Nick was entranced by the way her hair swung around her shoulders and gave off coppery-red sparks in the candlelight. "Aunt Jessie doesn't want to retire!"

"Oh, no? Have you asked her? Maybe she's been keeping Baker's afloat for your sake, not hers."

Callie stopped as if she'd run into a brick wall. That couldn't be true, could it? Again she shook her head in swift denial. "No," she said, nearly choking on the word, her voice barely a whisper. "No, she wouldn't do that. She loves Baker's as much as I do."

"I think," Nick said with a softness that surprised her, "that it's safe to say she loves you more than she loves Baker's."

Callie looked at him with stricken eyes. "What would she do, where would she go?"

"Maude has it in mind that she'll go to California to live."

"To Maude's?" Callie laughed at the absurdity of it. "That's crazy. They can't be in the same room for more than five minutes without fighting. Aunt Jessie would never agree to it."

Nick shifted uncomfortably, and Callie had the sudden impression, even through all the turmoil of her emotions, that the worst was yet to come. "Why don't you talk to Aunt Jessie about it?" he suggested.

"Oh, no you don't. You can't bring me this far along and just drop it. What do you know that I don't?"

Once more his eyes took on that resolute steeliness, and she marveled that she'd ever thought them warm and comforting. "Maude told me before I left California that all the arrangements had already been made. She said her sister Jessie was leaving Alaska and coming to live with her."

Callie bit down hard on her lip to keep from crying with pain and frustration. Control of her life seemed to have slipped into someone else's hands. "I don't believe you," she managed to say at last.

"Ask Aunt Jessie."

Callie grabbed her purse and got to her feet. "I will, right now."

This time Nick restrained her with a hand on her wrist. "Please sit down, Callie. It's late and she's probably sound asleep. Why don't we take this conversation down to the lounge? Our waiter looks like he's ready to go home."

What Nick said was true; their tuxedoed waiter was hovering nearby. Callie glanced around her and saw that the dining room had emptied while they'd talked. She knew the most sensible thing to do was to go home, but she wasn't ready to walk into her silent house with only her painful thoughts for company. "Okay," she agreed, and was rewarded with another one of his approving smiles.

Music, bluesy and bittersweet, flowed around them in the smoke-filled lounge. Callie loved music, especially the old standards this band favored, and she felt herself respond to it, willing it, at least for the time being, to melt away her anger and fear.

Nick's gaze rested expectantly on her face. "Would you like to dance?" he asked.

Callie looked across their small table and knew she should turn him down flat. He wasn't exactly her enemy, but he wasn't exactly her friend, either. Anyway, the only reason they were even there was to discuss Aunt Jessie's supposed move to California. But the sweet call of the music tugged at Callie again and she gave in to it. After all, what harm could one dance do? She nodded quickly before she could change her mind and pushed all her questions aside.

Nick led her out onto the dance floor and took her in his arms. At first she was stiff and awkward, holding herself away from him. But soon the music carried her away and she began to relax. She was tiny against his more-than-six-foot frame but still she fit, with her head tucked below his chin and one hand snuggled to his chest. "I love this song," she finally said with a sigh.

"It's by Irving Berlin, isn't it?"

She tilted her head back and looked up at him. "You know Irving Berlin?"

"Not personally," he teased, "but don't look so surprised. Even in the wilds of southern California, we've heard of him." And then Nick grew more serious. "I think you were born out of your time, Caledonia. The forties or maybe even the thirties would have suited you better."

"You're just saying that because of my dress."

"Maybe," he agreed easily, but she knew she hadn't convinced him.

Callie had told herself just one dance, but Nick had little trouble persuading her to dance another and then another until she was flushed and breathless with enjoyment. She didn't think of her troubles, choosing instead to give herself to the moment.

"Having fun?" Nick asked as they swayed to another heartbreak song, although it was obvious to anyone who looked at her that she was.

"The most fun I've had in years," she admitted with surprise. It didn't seem possible, but it was true. Even with her world crumbling around her, she found she was enjoying herself immensely.

"You know, Callie, you shouldn't bury yourself in antiques all the time."

"I don't."

"Don't you?" he countered.

"No. I have a life outside of Baker's."

"Like what?"

"Like . . . Aunt Jessie, the store, my house."

He shook his head. "Not enough. When was the last time you went dancing?"

It was admittedly a long time ago, longer than she cared to remember, but she wasn't going to tell *him* that. "I don't want to discuss my social life right now. All I want to do is dance."

Nick glanced down at her and sighed. "How can I resist when you look at me like that? Okay, no more serious talk."

"Scout's honor?"

He raised one hand. "Scout's honor," he said, and let his hand fall back to her waist.

Callie closed her eyes and leaned her head against his chest. She knew she should be fighting against the oddly tender feelings for this man that had come stealing into her heart. And she would. Tomorrow. But tonight was, well...tonight, and she wanted to savor every stolen moment.

They swayed together until they were the only ones left on the dance floor and even then Callie begged for one last song. The band leader, a romantic at heart, agreed. "What will it be, folks?"

Nick smiled down at Callie for a moment and then turned to the band. "Anything by Irving Berlin."

Without hesitation the leader nodded and gestured to his musicians. At the first note, Nick pulled Callie close and rested his head on hers. They slowly circled the dance floor, completely lost in time.

The night was bright with stars, the air cold and biting as they pulled to a halt about a half a block away from Callie's house and climbed from Nick's rental car. Sassafras Street lay deserted before them, its stores shuttered and dark. But street lamps lit their way, casting pools of golden light on the red brick sidewalk with its scattered patches of snow and ice.

It seemed the most natural thing in the world for Nick to put his arm around Callie's shoulders as they walked toward her house. And even more natural for him to pause on the doorstep and take her in his arms. "I've enjoyed myself this evening," he said, his head bent to hers.

Callie could only nod. She found she couldn't speak over the mad pounding of her heart. The moonlight had hollowed and defined his face, giving him the dark, dangerous look of a pirate. She knew with a certainty then, that she wasn't any more secure from his marauding ways than the store had been.

She tried to shake off the sensation. "We'll really have to get down to work tomorrow," she managed to say as she made a grab for reality.

He seemed amused. "So we will. But I do have one more serious thing to do before this evening's over."

"What's that?" she whispered, as breathless as a tropical day. His face turned even more hawklike, and Callie had only an instant to once again think he belonged at the helm of a pirate ship. He lowered his head then, until his breath fanned dark and sweet over her cheek and stirred the tendrils of her hair. Against her will, she closed her eyes and with parted lips, raised her face to his.

"Just this," he said and pressed a fleeting kiss on her forehead.

If Callie had ever wondered if it were possible to feel two completely opposite emotions at the same time, that kiss settled the question. She was both relieved and supremely disappointed he hadn't kissed her on the mouth.

Nick's low voice caught at her as she turned away from him and let herself in the front door. "Good night, Caledonia."

Without looking back, Callie paused. "Good night, Nick," she said, voice trembling, and shut the door. She leaned against the safety of the closed door, heart pounding. From the other side she could just hear the sound of Nick's soft laughter.

## Chapter Three

It was past eleven when Callie reached the shop the next morning. "Aunt Jessie, I'm sorry I'm late," she began, hastily pulling off her coat and boots and putting them away. "I overslept." What she didn't say was that she'd been out dancing with Nick until the wee hours of the morning and had consequently had trouble getting out of bed.

Aunt Jessie bustled by her, intent on the full bowl of cream she held in her hands. "No matter, my dear. The store has been very quiet. And actually I enjoyed having a chance to get to know Nick. He's quite a nice young man, isn't he?" This last came from the depths of the armoire as Aunt Jessie set the bowl of cream inside.

Nice? Maybe, Callie thought. When he wanted to be. But that wasn't the word she would choose to describe him. *Dangerous* seemed more apt. She shrugged the thought away and leaned against the massive piece of furniture. "Aunt Jessie, Nick told me something very strange last night."

Her aunt straightened up. "What's that, my dear?"

Callie took a deep breath. "He said you're going to go live with Aunt Maude in California. I told him that was the most ridiculous thing I've ever heard."

Aunt Jessie's china-blue eyes slid away from Callie's. "No, Callie dear, I don't find that ridiculous. California is a beautiful place. I've always said so."

Callie knew her aunt had the maddening habit of keeping any news she considered less than happy to herself. "You didn't answer my question, Aunt Jessie."

The other woman fiddled with the rhinestone brooch pinned to her shirtfront. "Actually, my dear, you didn't ask me one."

"Aunt Jessie, please, tell me the truth. Are you going to live with Aunt Maude?"

Aunt Jessie touched Callie gently on the cheek, her gaze now direct and sharp. "Yes, dear, I am. I think it's for the best."

"How can it be? I know you and Maude have never gotten along well." She paused, fighting back a sudden rush of emotion. "And besides," she finally went on as she battled for control, "I don't want you to go."

"Of course, you don't, that's only natural. Why, you've been the daughter I never had. But it's time for you to be out on your own. All birds must fly the nest sometime."

"Then *I'll* leave, find another job. Just don't go, Aunt Jessie."

"There, there, dear, don't you worry your head about me," Aunt Jessie soothed, wrapping her niece in a warm embrace. "California is not so very far away. You'll come to see me all the time. And, of course, I'll come back here for visits. But for now, I've got some fences that need mending and not so very much time left to me in which to do it."

Callie searched Aunt Jessie's beloved, time-worn face and saw for the first time how truly old she had grown. "I'll come with you," she said, fear clutching at her heart.

"You'll do no such thing. You must stay here and help Nick run the store. I'd hate to see it close down after all these years. It's been our lives for a very long time, Callie, and it's worth saving."

Callie knew that as soft as Aunt Jessie appeared, she was implacable when her mind was made up. But even as Callie gave in, she felt a faint stirring of resentment. Not at Aunt Jessie, of course. But at a fate, in the shape of Nick Logan, which had turned her life inside out.

Aunt Jessie watched as acceptance slowly settled over Callie's features. "Good girl," she said approvingly, and then with one of her blithe smiles, "You never know, you might even find yourself enjoying the whole situation. After all, Nick is a very attractive young man, don't you think so?''

Yes, Callie thought, any fool could see he was attractive. But he was hardly the kind of man she wanted to become romantically involved with. She was sure that would only lead to heartache. "I'll do all this, Aunt Jessie, everything you want me to, but only if you promise me no more matchmaking."

Aunt Jessie's laughter tinkled with silvery delight. "I'm very sure, Callie dearest, that my work is already done. Now, run along and find Nick. He said he wanted to see you as soon as you came in."

Callie sighed with resignation. She knew when she'd met her match. "Anything you say, Aunt Jessie." But confronting Nick, especially after last night, was not going to be easy. She'd decided long after she'd turned out her lights and given up on ever getting to sleep, that a romance with him would just never do. By a twist of fate they were business associates, but that was where it ended. No more dinners out, and certainly no more dancing wrapped in each other's arms to long, slow songs that seemed to never end. She shivered suddenly. No, most definitely, no more of that.

Now she needed to tell him of her decision. She was sure he would see how sensible it was. He was a reasonable man, just as she was a reasonable woman. They would establish a good working relationship and keep it at that. For the sake of the store.

She found him hard at word at the desk. "Nick? I have something I'd like to say." But when he turned those blue eyes of his on her, she forgot for a moment what it was.

"Hi," he said, giving her a lazy smile. "Sleep well?"

Why did he make a simple question sound so full of innuendo? "No," she said more sharply than she had intended. "That is, just fine, thank you," she amended, striving for a brisk, businesslike tone but sounding, to her own ears, almost peevish instead. This was not starting out well.

He leaned back in the chair and clasped his arms behind his head. "I had a good time last night."

"Nick," she began again, determined to say her piece, but he interrupted her.

"We'll have to do it again. Soon."

For just a second she could feel his arms around her once more, hear the smoky music with its heartbreak lyrics and she wavered. What harm could it really do? Plenty, an inward voice cautioned, and she recovered her senses. "Look, Nick," she said quickly, "I don't think it's a very good idea for us to socialize after work. After all, we've got quite a job to do here and we both need clear minds to see it through."

"Clear minds," he echoed, that lazy smile still curving his mouth. "Yes, I think you could be right. Dancing has been known to inflame people into doing horrible things, like having fun, relaxing, blowing off a little steam, you know, crazy, unpredictable things like that. No, running an antique business calls for absolute lucidity."

"Good. We agree then," she said, uncertain if they did at all.

"Oh, absolutely. You know what they say about work."

"No, unless it's 'All work and no play...'"

"'...Makes Jack a dull boy,'" he finished for her, his grin growing wicked. "No, it has some merit, but I was thinking of something else, something I had to learn in school. 'Work-work-work till the brain begins to swim; work-work-work till the eyes are heavy and dim.'" He grinned suddenly, the very devil himself in that smile. "It's been my motto for many years, and look where it's gotten me."

"Right," she said, sure now that she was being teased but refusing to rise to the bait. "I'm glad you agree with me." Or at least she thought he agreed with her. She shoved out her hand. "Let's shake on it."

That was a mistake. As soon as he took her hand in his, those tingling sensations flowed up her arm again, and she felt her breath grow shallow and weak. Nick held her hand longer than he should have, and it seemed as if he knew what effect he was having on her for his face held an intent expression as he studied her.

It was his air of almost predatory concentration that finally lent her the strength of will to pull free of him. She didn't like to play games and it was obvious to her that was what he was doing. "Aunt Jessie said you wanted to see me," she said sharply.

"I do. Let's go for a tour of the neighborhood."

"Okay," she agreed readily. For some reason, the close confines of the store were making her uneasy.

"Just let me get my coat and tell Aunt Jessie where we're going."

He met her by the front door a few minutes later and ushered her outside. "Where to first?" he asked.

"Leoni's," she said without hesitation. "It's the restaurant right across the street."

"Good, I'm starved. I'll treat you to lunch."

"Dutch treat," she insisted. "You don't need to buy lunch for me."

"What if I said it was my pleasure?"

I'd say you have a golden tongue, Nick Logan, she thought. "Then I could hardly refuse," she said instead, and switched the subject to more neutral ground. "Leoni is famous for her pies."

Nick linked his arm through hers. "You mean there really is a Leoni?"

Callie wished he hadn't put his arm through hers. Close contact with him seemed to sharpen her senses and fuzz her mind when what she wanted was exactly the opposite. "Just like there's a Donaldson at the dry-goods store and a Baker at the antique store."

"I like that. It's quaint."

He had an aptitude for putting her on the defensive. "I'm not sure I like being called 'quaint.'"

"You, Caledonia, are far from quaint."

And an equal knack for making her feel vulnerable, she thought, shivering at the faint growl in his voice.

They walked the rest of the way to Leoni's in silence. But as soon as they entered the spacious café with its red-checked tablecloths and stained-glass fixtures, it was Leoni herself who forced them into conversation again. A petite woman with hair piled to an impossible height, she was yelling orders at a small army of waitresses from her vantage point at the cash register. "Don't forget the rolls," she called to the scurrying women. "If I've told you once, I've told you a million times, don't forget the rolls."

"That's Leoni," Callie explained in a whisper to Nick. "She's a true martinet, but everyone, including all those waitresses, really loves her. She's probably lent money to half of them and stands as godmother to most of their kids."

Nick shook his head in disbelief as Leoni started in on yet another tirade, this time about the menus. "Don't leave those menus on the table," she shouted toward one hapless waitress. "Looks tacky."

Callie could feel Nick's shoulders begin to heave with silent mirth. "Don't you dare laugh," she cautioned him. "Leoni might not ever forgive you."

Leoni chose that moment to level a long, appraising look their way. And then, menus tacked under her arm, she strode toward them. "Callie," she called, "who is that gorgeous man you've got with you? Boyfriend, I hope, and about time, too."

Utter silence reigned throughout the restaurant as dozens of customers and every waitress took the time to survey Leoni's latest victims.

At that point, Callie could have dug a six-foot-deep trench in the floor and climbed in. But, of course, there was no escape. It was just too bad she'd forgotten Leoni's unfortunate habit of conducting all business at a bellow. "Leoni Wilkins," she managed to say calmly as the woman halted in front of them, "I'd like you to meet Nick Logan. He's the new manager of Baker's. Maude sent him."

Leoni, eyes bright with undisguised curiosity, turned to Nick. "What's the old biddy up to now?" she shouted.

Callie noted that he gave Leoni the smile he seemed to reserve for old women and kittens, the same one that turned them to putty in his hands. He'd never directed one like it at her, she thought. The smiles he tossed in her direction were decidedly less angelic.

"Why don't you join us for lunch," he asked Leoni, "and I'll be able to fill you in on the particulars."

Leoni was no fool. She knew when she was being managed, but her curiosity was all consuming. "Never eat lunch," she yelled, "but I'll have a cup of tea while you do." She turned and, at almost a dead run, led the way to a narrow booth overlooking Sassafras Street.

Nick slid into the booth next to Callie and smiled across at Leoni. "Nice place you have here."

Leoni looked around her with satisfaction. "I like it."

A waitress approached them, pen poised to take their orders. "Bring two specials," Leoni barked without consulting either Nick or Callie, "and a cup of tea for me."

Nick shared a glance with Callie. "Chicken," she mouthed.

He cocked a questioning eyebrow at her.

"It's Tuesday," she murmured.

"Now," Leoni said, her voice dropping to what passed as a whisper for her, "give."

"I can count on your discretion?"

For all her thundering locution, Leoni could be discreet when she wanted to be. "Naturally," she said, her voice falling another decibel.

"Among other reasons, I'm here at Maude Baker's request to assess the business climate of Sassafras Street."

"That's doublespeak if I've ever heard it," Leoni snorted, voice rising. "Give, boy, and don't try to fool an old woman like me. I've been around long enough to hear every line of bull there is. Twice."

Nick grinned. "I'm here to make Baker's a going concern."

Leoni nodded. "It's about time, too. Now, Callie, don't give me those fish eyes. You know darned good and well you and Jessie need some help from that boiled old owl you call an aunt. Everybody up and down the block has been sprucing things up. You know, new interiors, new storefronts. New businesses in long-empty buildings. Baker's could stand some of the same."

"Has business increased lately with the gentrification of the block?" Nick rested his elbows on the table and leaned toward Leoni, intent on her answer.

"The what?" Leoni asked suspiciously.

"Gentrification," Nick repeated patiently. "It means exactly what's been going on here on Sassafras Street. New businesses coming in, old businesses with new life."

Leoni nodded so vigorously, her tall beehive hairdo wobbled precariously. "Whatever it is, a face-lift or this gentrifi-whatchamacallit, it's working. My business is up. Donaldson, down at the dry-goods store, he'll have to tell you himself, but I think he's up. So's The Corner Emporium."

Their food arrived just at that moment and Leoni slipped back into her public persona, that of full-tongued termagant. "The rolls," she boomed to the waitress. "What did I say about the rolls?"

The waitress grinned at Nick and Callie. "Be back in a minute, folks, with your rolls."

Nick actually laughed, and Leoni fixed him with a baleful eye. "I make those blasted things myself, but the girls keep forgetting to bring them out. They're not doing any good sitting in the kitchen."

"Oh, I agree," Nick said solemnly. "I can't wait to taste what I'm sure is a culinary masterpiece."

It was Leoni's turn to laugh. "He's a smooth customer, Callie. I'd hang on to him if I were you."

Callie almost choked on a piece of chicken. "Really, Leoni," she said earnestly when she could manage to speak again, "we're not, I mean, he's not . . ."

Leoni reached over and patted her on the hand. "Then he should be, Callie," she cried for the edification of the entire restaurant. "He's a keeper, if I've ever seen one."

Why was it, Callie thought, subsiding in mortification, that both Leoni and Aunt Jessie seemed so intent on marrying her off to a man who was totally wrong for her? It was beginning to drive her crazy.

She glanced over at Nick and caught his eye. For just a heartbeat, the denizens of Leoni's faded away and she and Nick were alone. Nick didn't touch her or even smile at her, but the look he gave her was so intimate, she felt as if he were holding her in his arms again. She knew then she would have to stand guard over her foolish heart.

From her side of the table, Leoni took it all in. With a grunt of satisfaction, she climbed to her feet and nodded her head wisely. "And for your part, Mr. Logan," she said in a surprisingly gentle voice when he turned to look at her, "you'll not find a better one than our Callie here. Eat up," she concluded with a bellow. "My biscuits aren't getting any younger."

Nick started to laugh, and Callie didn't think he was going to stop. "Do I need to hit you on the back?" she asked as tears began to slide from his eyes.

He shook his head and finally managed to get his amusement under control. "She's wonderful," he gasped, using his napkin to wipe at his eyes.

Callie's answering smile was so dubious, Nick burst into a fresh paroxysm of laughter. "Now what's so funny?" she asked.

"Not funny," he answered. "Delightful. I've never met anyone quite like the residents of Sassafras Street before."

"You make it sound like we're curiosities in a sideshow."

"No, not curiosities. Genuine people, without a single pretense. So when I say I've never met anyone like you, I mean it as a compliment. Everything you feel, you feel passionately. I'm tired of people who do things because they're expected to do them or feel things because they're expected to feel them.''

''If you dislike people like that so much, why do you keep their company?''

He smiled. ''See how easy the solution is for you? If you don't like the company you keep, change it. Well, it's not as easy as all that.''

Not anymore, she agreed with silent irony.

''To be a success in a high-profile, highly competitive business,'' he went on, ''you have to play the game. And the game includes an endless round of cocktail parties, banquets and receptions. It means—'' and his mouth twisted slightly ''—currying favor with people you would rather not deal with.''

She realized that here, at least in part, was one of the things over which he and his father must have disagreed. ''Our problems must seem pretty clear-cut and easy to solve to you.''

''They are. They're mine that have gotten more difficult.''

''What problems are those?''

He gave her a troubled look. ''I could mention the beautiful woman whose place I've usurped, the nice little old lady who has to leave her home or,'' he added with a touch of dry humor, ''the macho instincts that led me into buying a very expensive necklace I didn't know I wanted.'' He covered her hand with his. ''Look, Callie, I'm not completely insensitive. I know this is hard on both you and your Aunt Jessie.'' And then his eyes became hooded. ''But it's a job I wanted and one I'll see through to the end. I told you once, Callie, I always get what I want, no matter what the consequences.''

She looked down at where her hand lay hidden beneath his in such a natural way, almost as though it belonged there. Hastily she pulled it free and tucked it into her lap. ''Maybe we should finish here and continue our tour. I—I told Aunt Jessie we wouldn't be gone too long,'' she managed to stammer.

Mouth twisted with amusement, Nick looked from her hand to his and then into her face. But she studiously avoided meeting his eyes. He could be amused all he desired, but she didn't want him to touch her. She didn't need to give him a reason why.

After they'd paid their bill and bid Leoni farewell, they walked on up Sassafras Street, stopping in every shop. A few of the newer merchants didn't know Callie, but everyone else did, and Nick saw that she was an obvious favorite with them. More than one of them made her blush with stories of watching her grow from an awkward teen to a lovely woman.

''It's obvious,'' Nick finally said after they'd finished touring the last thriving businesses, ''that Baker's is located in a healthy economic environment.''

''So,'' she surmised, ''you'll want to go ahead with the remodeling.''

''Yes,'' he agreed, and there was more than a measure of relief in his voice.

''What would the alternative have been?''

''To liquidate,'' he said shortly.

She winced at the harshness of the answer. No matter what the circumstances, anything was preferable to closing down the store for good.

Once back at Baker's, Nick called a conference among the three of them. He waited with the patience he seemed to reserve just for Aunt Jessie until she had seen to Shadow, fixed them all a cup of tea and fussed over a first-time customer who was in the shop "just to browse." And then Nick coaxed her to sit down in a comfortable ladder-back rocking chair and put her feet on a small footstool.

"Just for a minute," she chirped. "I've got so much to do today."

"Why don't you come sit by me?" Nick said to Callie, and with a flourish, plucked a handkerchief from his pants pocket and made a great show of dusting off a rickety old chair he'd set much too close to his for her own comfort.

Having found out just how perilous it was to get near him, Callie sat down gingerly and held herself stiffly erect.

He draped his arm along the back of her chair and let his fingertips brush through the stray tendrils of her hair one too many times for the action to be accidental. She shifted uncomfortably and tried to sit even straighter, but she could still feel that gentle sensation of him playing with her hair. She wanted to tell him to stop. But she knew him well enough already to realize he would somehow deny he was doing anything to bother her and she would be the one to end up looking like a fool.

"Aunt Jessica," Nick began without preamble, "I've decided to keep the store going."

"I'm so glad to hear that." Aunt Jessie's face sagged with relief, and Callie realized that the possibility of the store being closed was not a new one to her aunt. She wondered then if her aunt was keeping anything else unpleasant to herself.

"I do feel that we'll have to close temporarily, however, for remodeling," Nick went on. "Would the end of the week be too soon for you?"

Callie wondered if she would ever understand him. Just when she thought she had him figured out, he turned into a different person. She'd been so sure he was an autocrat of the worst sort, but then he'd deferred to Aunt Jessie in such a thoughtful way, and she wasn't so sure any longer.

"No, no," Aunt Jessie answered. "That will be just fine. Now if you children don't need me any longer, I think I might run on upstairs and go through a few of my things. It seems as if I'm going to be moving very soon."

Nick helped her to her feet. "Are you sure you don't want to be in on some of the planning sessions for the remodeling?"

She patted him gently on the cheek. "My, my, no. I'll leave that all up to the two of you. And I'm not matchmaking," she said, turning to Callie.

Of course, you are, Callie thought, feeling the telltale color flood her cheeks again. "Thank you, Aunt Jessie," she said instead. "I'll come up and see you as soon as I'm done."

"No hurry, dear. You stay down here and enjoy yourself. And that's not matchmaking, either," she said quickly before Callie had a chance to protest, and just as quickly climbed the stairs to her apartment.

Nick glanced over at Callie. "What was that all about?"

"Never mind," she muttered. "Just a little joke with Aunt Jessie." Some joke, she added inwardly, wishing for that six-foot-deep trench again.

"Tell me, Callie," he asked, settling back into his chair, "what would you do to Baker's if it were yours?"

She knew it was important to choose her words carefully. She loved Baker's, but that hadn't blinded her to its need for some cosmetic surgery. And she had a few cherished notions about what it required. "First of all, I'd pick a color scheme, pinks mostly with blue accents. The walls should be wainscoted in cherry wood with a small floral print wallcovering above. Chandeliers, of course, probably stained glass, rose-colored carpet, miniblinds and lace curtains at the window."

"Sounds nice," Nick commented. "Now get realistic."

"What do you mean, 'get realistic'?" she said, bristling. "It would make a perfect setting for the antiques. Elegant, Victorian—"

"Expensive, impractical," he finished for her.

Callie flushed hotly. "What do you have in mind, drab browns, track lighting, glass and chrome."

It was his turn to be defensive. "There's nothing wrong with being functional."

There was no need to worry about losing her heart to Nick Logan. He was completely insufferable! "You'd ruin the whole atmosphere of the store with that. People want elegance."

"Elegance maybe, but not all the fluff and foof you have in mind."

She had to take a deep steadying breath to keep from grabbing up a nearby parasol and bopping him over the head. He was such a pigheaded man. There was no way they could ever work together to run this store. "It seems we have nothing further to say to each other," she snapped, getting to her feet.

"You're going to have to learn to compromise, Callie."

If ever there was a case of the pot calling the kettle black, this was it. "And do it all your way, right? Some compromise."

He shifted uncomfortably as her words hit home. "Okay," he finally said, "you've made your point. Now, why don't you sit down and see if we can hammer out some workable solution."

If he'd only railed at her, she could have walked away, righteous indignation intact. But as it was, his very willingness to be reasonable prompted the same response in her. "Well," she said, sitting down again, "maybe pink carpet would be a little hard to keep clean."

He had the good sense not to smile. "What about gray, something neutral without being too light."

"I like it," she said slowly. "It would look good with pink."

"I don't like the pink, Callie. It's too much the color of a woman's boudoir." He held up his hand to stop her immediate flow of words. "Not that I have anything against a woman's boudoir. In fact..." That predatory look came back into his eyes as he probed hers. "Well, never mind about that," he went on with an amused smile as soon as her suddenly pink cheeks announced she was fully aware of his meaning. "But what about going with blue instead?"

She had an immediate objection. "Too cold of a color. Remember, winter lasts for nine months up here. The predominate colors outside are blue and white. We need something warm and inviting."

"Such as?" he prompted.

She thought for a moment. It was hard to visualize anything different from her long-cherished dreams. As she glanced around the store, searching for inspiration, her eye was caught by a shaft of sunlight slanting in through the front window. That was it. Perfect. "Yellow," she said, excited by the concept. "It would be great with the gray carpet, bright, and a good background for all the wooden furniture."

He nodded, caught up in her excitement. "What about red for an accent color?"

She almost said no. Red seemed too garish to her. But he looked so pleased with himself and after all, he'd been willing to go along with her. "Great," she told him, almost meaning it. "I can see it now. Geraniums in the windows, country accents here and there, maybe braided rugs in some of the different areas. We've got lots of ruby-glass pieces we can feature throughout the store,'' she went on, warming to the idea, ''and some old bricks we can pile up for display stands.''

''We'll drop the ceiling and put in track lighting,'' he added enthusiastically.

''No, that would be wrong.''

''What's wrong with it?'' he demanded, voice rising.

She missed the warning signal. ''It's too modern, that's what's wrong with it.''

He ran his hand through his hair in exasperation. ''Callie, this place is a barn. You can't see anything the way it is now. And the heating bills are atrocious. Something has to give.''

She wasn't going to be the something. ''Track lighting is too modern,'' she insisted, holding her ground. ''It would clash with the rest of the store.''

''Okay. What if we dropped the ceiling, hung some period piece lighting fixtures, say in either the Art Nouveau or Art Deco style, and put in some sort of wall sconces in the areas where we need more light.''

''It might work,'' she said slowly, once more readjusting her mental picture of the store.

''Not might, will,'' he insisted. ''I'll do some of the scale drawing while you put together the colors. You know, swatches of fabric, paint chips, wallpaper samples.''

''Okay,'' she said, getting to her feet.

''Just okay?'' he demanded.

She couldn't help but smile. "Better than okay. It sounds like fun."

"Good. Let's shake on it."

He thrust his hand out at her, but she was wise now to what taking his hand would do to her. She shoved her hands into her jean pockets and took a step backward. "No, that's okay. We have a deal."

Nick stood up. "I make it a point to seal any deals I make," he said, advancing on her.

"We—we don't need to," she stammered, backing even further away.

"Oh yes, we do," he said, and took a step closer to her. "But I've noticed that you don't like shaking hands. Perhaps something a little more genteel would suit you better."

She didn't think she liked the all-too-familiar glint she saw in his eyes. She stepped backward again and ran up against the edge of a solidly built oak bookcase. "What did you have in mind?"

"I thought you'd never ask." And before she had a chance to react, he leaned over and brushed a kiss across her lips. "Do we have a deal?" he asked, eyes now softening to a tender blue.

Callie could only nod. For when his mouth had touched hers, he had set her on fire. And she knew, deep within her, the flames would never be put out.

## Chapter Four

Callie looked over Nick's shoulder at the scale drawing he'd done of the store. "Well, what do you think?" he asked.

Her eyes drifted to the back of his head. It was hard to think when she was so close to him, when she had to focus all her concentration to keep her hands from reaching out and touching his black, satin hair, curling her fingers in its softness. To keep from telling him . . . telling him what?

To never kiss her again, she answered silently. For the past week as she'd gone about her task of coordinating the palette of colors they were going to use in the store, she'd been able to think of little else besides that kiss.

"Callie?"

"Hmm?"

"Don't you like it?"

She snapped back to the present. "It's fine."

He swiveled around so that now she was staring into those hypnotic blue eyes of his. "Fine? Is that all you can say?"

"It's good. Great. Wonderful," she said, letting irritation creep into her voice as she wrenched her own eyes away from his. She didn't like the effect he had on her. Whenever he looked at her or talked to her or even got close to her, she grew thick in the head and weak in the knees.

"Let's see what you've got," he said mildly. Fortunately for her, he seemed to accept her quick-changing moods as normal. But even that galled her. She wanted to tell him how even tempered she usually was, how sunny natured, how unmoody. But then she would also have to explain it was his presence that seemed to cause her to be so...so capricious. Happy one minute, angry the next, inexplicably close to tears after that.

She fanned her array of paint chips and fabric swatches out in front of him, pleased, even through her discomfort, with how good they all looked together. Aunt Jessie had approved her every choice and was upstairs flipping through wallpaper books now, thoroughly enjoying her newfound leisure time to "putter," as she called it.

"The red I chose is on the orange side," Callie explained. "I like the way it contrasts so vividly with both the yellow and the gray."

He shuffled through the sample pieces without a word.

"Well?" she finally asked.

"They're fine."

"Is that all?" she demanded, and then laughed. Of course he was teasing her, giving her a taste of her own medicine. "It's going to be beautiful, isn't it?"

He leaned back and grinned with satisfaction. "I think so. But now comes the hard part."

"What's that?"

"First, we move all the stock into the middle of the floor and cover it with drop cloths. That will take the rest of the day. Then we tear into the actual remodeling. I've already gotten the necessary construction permits, so we can start that tomorrow."

"Let's do it, then," she said, anxious to begin. Maybe some good hard physical activity would shake her out of this adolescent woolgathering she'd been caught up in for the past few days.

Together they shifted boxes of knickknacks away from the walls, moved furniture, rolled up rugs and draped breakables. It was every bit as hard as Nick had promised, but even as she sweated and groaned, Callie still found her thoughts drifting back to that fleeting kiss a week ago.

Had it meant any more to him than what he'd said it was, a way to seal their bargain? He certainly hadn't tried to do it again. But in all honesty, she hadn't created many opportunities for it, either. Whenever he got close enough to even think of puckering up, she was on the run, scurrying to a far corner of the store on some trumped up errand.

It's not like I want him to kiss me again, she'd told herself while she'd stood trembling in her corner. In fact, that was the last thing she wanted. What she desired above all else was a return to the peace and serenity of her life before Nick Logan had entered it.

"Callie?"

"What?"

"Is something wrong?"

"No, why?"

"You've been standing there holding that umbrella stand for a good five minutes."

Callie looked down at the battered copper umbrella stand as if seeing it for the first time. "I have?"

"Just put it down right there," he instructed her. "Maybe it's time for a break."

"I could use one," she agreed, carefully setting the umbrella stand at her feet and leaning over to rub her suddenly aching back muscles. "I hurt in places I didn't even know I had."

"Here, let me," Nick said, and before she could go into her usual disappearing act, he was massaging her back with firm, all-too-sensuous strokes.

She wanted to stop him, but she couldn't. Not when his fingers were working such magic on her sore back. Not when her blood began to flow through her body like thick, sweet molasses and every word died on her lips. She closed her eyes and moaned with pleasure.

"Feel good?" he asked, his own voice husky.

"Mmm," she sighed. "Wonderful."

Nick leaned closer to her until his breath stirred her hair. "Why don't we grab a bite to eat before we do any more?"

His words were perfectly ordinary; nothing suggestive about them. Then why was it they caused something inside of her to do a stomach-wrenching somersault? "Dinner sounds great," she murmured, knowing she should head, instead, for one of her corner hiding places.

"Leoni's?"

"Where else?"

"I'll get our coats."

After he left, she stood unmoving for a long moment. Okay, she told herself sternly, so you're attracted to him. That's only natural; he's an attractive man. But he's an arrogant, impossible one, too. Stay away, my girl, she warned herself once again. He's at Baker's for only one reason, and it's not you. But somewhere along the line, about the time of his last kiss, the admonition had lost its urgency and she was having a great deal of trouble getting it back.

"Callie, I told you that day at the auction you should never play high-stakes poker."

She blinked and found Nick standing in front of her. "What do you mean?"

"I mean you look like you're giving yourself quite a tongue-lashing. Either that, or planning to give it to someone else."

"I was just clarifying a few things in my mind."

"Like what?"

Not wanting to confess the continuing battle between her heart and her good sense, she blurted out the first thing that had come to mind. "Like—like how a walk before dinner might be fun." Nice one, she thought with an inward groan. If she really wanted some distance from him, an intimate stroll down Anchorage's byways was no way to find it.

"Sounds good to me," he agreed readily, and slipped his arm through hers.

There was nothing for Callie to do but grin and bear it. They left the store behind and tramped down Sassafras Street, turning a corner into the quiet residential block that bordered it. Callie gazed up into the darkening sky and inhaled deeply, savoring the achingly clear evening air. Twilight was always her favorite time of day, but tonight it was beautiful beyond belief. And then it suddenly struck her. It was so spectacular because for the first time in her life, she had someone to share it with. The wrong someone, she added sadly.

They stopped by mutual consent in a clearing and stared over the restless waters of Cook Inlet to the far distant mountains of the Alaska Range. The dying sun touched their craggy peaks with fire and Callie thought, as she often did, that if paradise could be found on earth, it would be in those pristine mountains. "It's beautiful here," she said, as much to herself as to him.

"Yes, it is," he said, but his eyes were focused far closer to home than the blue-shadowed mountains across the water.

Callie shivered. Her unruly feelings for him set alarm bells ringing in her head and it was high time she got a firm hold on her galloping emotions. She and Nick had been thrown together under what, for her at least, were extremely stressful circumstances. Any strong feelings she had for him, and they seemed to swing wildly from something more than like to something more than dislike, had to be discounted. "Let's go eat," she said shortly. "I'm starved."

The trip to Leoni's took place in silence, but if Nick felt any of the strain Callie was undergoing, he didn't say so.

Once they were seated in the bustling restaurant, it was Leoni herself who waited on their table. "What'll it be?" she asked, managing even with the mundane words to sound coy as she glanced from Nick's face to Callie's.

"The special, what else?" Nick answered promptly with a conspiratorial wink in Callie's direction.

"You've got the special," Leoni wisecracked, nodding at Callie.

Callie wanted to dive under the table. The last thing she needed was this determined, if unlikely, fairy godmother. "I'll have the roast beef special, too," she muttered, hoping Leoni would go away as soon as she had their order.

No such luck. Under her tough exterior, Leoni Wilkins was a born romantic and she wasn't about to let the matter drop. "Darla," she shouted over her shoulder at one of the scurrying waitresses, "we need a candle over here." And then to Nick and Callie in a voice that could be heard two blocks away, she said, "You gotta have candlelight if you're going to fall in love."

Callie didn't just want to climb under the table now, she wanted to flatten herself out and become a part of the linoleum. "Leoni, what are you doing?" she ground out.

"Giving old mother nature a nudge, that's all," the other woman answered. "Now, straighten up, here comes Darla."

Callie sat in red-faced silence as Darla produced a candle and Leoni lit it with a dramatic flourish. And even after the two women had gone, Callie still had trouble meeting Nick's gaze. "Both Aunt Jessie and Leoni have been trying to marry me off for years," she finally offered in the lengthening silence.

"Why haven't they succeeded?"

At last Callie met his frank blue eyes. "Let's see," she reflected, a wry smile touching her lips, "first there was the plumber's son, but he didn't like me any better than I liked him. And then there was the nephew of a friend of a friend. He was nice enough but he was seven years younger than I was and told me I looked like his mother." Callie shook her head sadly. "That didn't do much for the old ego. And then there was Leoni's new cook. His views on women include bare feet and lots of babies."

Laughing, Nick held up his hand to stop her. "Are you sure they don't know my mother? This sounds like a list of my own blind dates. I swear she has built-in radar for any unattached female within a hundred miles.''

Callie was fascinated. He sounded so human all of a sudden with a matchmaking mother and a string of blind dates. ''She never found you the right one?''

''Nope. How about you?''

''Nope,'' she echoed. ''Not yet.''

As if on cue, Leoni reappeared at their table bearing two plates of roast beef and a surprise bottle of wine. ''My treat,'' she explained, pouring them each a glass. ''Gotta have wine with the candlelight.''

''Thank you, Leoni,'' Callie said quickly in hopes of staving off any more references to old mother nature and young love.

But Leoni was caught up in her dreams of romance. ''I would have had some violins play for you two lovebirds, but the best I could do was a harmonica.''

''No, Leoni, you don't understand. We don't...that is I don't... Really, this is too much,'' Callie finished, an edge of hysteria entering in her voice.

Ignoring her, Leoni clapped her hands and the cook appeared, his face impassive under his traditional white hat. ''I've only got one song,'' he told them. ''But first I want to say good luck to you.'' His sympathetic eyes on Nick's face said he thought the other man would need it. '' 'Oh, Susanna,' '' he announced, deadpan, and launched into an off-key rendition.

Callie couldn't look at Nick. But she knew from the strangled noises coming at her from across the table, he was having trouble holding back his mirth. At last the song ended, and in a gracious gesture, Nick picked up his wineglass and toasted the cook and Leoni. "Thank you both," he said gravely, although his eyes danced with barely suppressed laughter. "I, for one, will never forget this evening."

Satisfied, Leoni ordered the cook back to the kitchen. "You can't be dawdling out here all day," she bawled. "We've got people to feed." And with his face still impassive, the cook bowed quickly and strode back to his domain.

"Enjoy, kids," Leoni commanded, and then she, too, hurried off to once more harass her waitresses.

"Is that by any chance the same cook who wanted you barefoot and..."

"The same one," Callie said quickly.

Nick grinned. "He's quite a musician. Maybe you need to reconsider."

"Judging from the look he gave you, I don't think he'd have me."

Nick lifted his wineglass to her. "Then he's a fool," he said softly and took a drink from his glass.

Callie ducked her head and dug into her meal. His comment was the natural reply of a practiced flirt, which he was, of course. But it had the same peculiar effect on her heart as his touch did, causing it to lurch and sway in the most disconcerting fashion. "Eat up," she mumbled. "Leoni may not be done with us yet. We might want to make a hasty getaway."

Nick laughed. "I hate to think what might be next."

"She does seem to have all the bases covered, soft music, good wine, candlelight—"

"Don't look now," Nick broke in, "but I think she's got one more surprise." Both of them watched with fascination as Leoni bore down on them, a giant corsage clutched in her hand. Somehow she'd found the world's largest pom-pom mum and had decided it was the pièce de résistance the evening needed.

"Every girl loves flowers," she said, giving Nick an accusatory glance, as if he should have thought of it himself. "For you, Callie," she added, handing her the corsage with a flourish.

It took two hands to hold the huge mum. "Leoni, what can I say? Words fail me."

"No thanks needed. Now, young man, you slide in right next to Callie and pin this flower on her. I gotta get back to work." With that, Leoni was off to terrorize another waitress or two.

"I think I should do as she asks," Nick said.

"You don't strike me as a man who does what he's told."

"I do what I'm told—" he paused for emphasis "—only when I want to." He slipped into the booth next to her then and took the corsage from her. She caught her breath as he slid his hand in at the open neck of her blouse and pinned the flower in place. Just the feel of his fingers barely brushing her skin was enough to fan the flames of her desire again.

The corsage firmly in place, Nick raised his head and found Callie's mouth a few scant inches from his own. "Hi," he murmured.

"Hi," she whispered, breathless.

"Your flower should stay on now."

"Thank you."

"Anything else I can do for you?"

"I can't think of a thing." Actually she could, but she wasn't about to say so and spend the next week in the same state of turmoil in which she'd spent the past one.

"Pity. We'll have to work on your imagination, Caledonia." He gave her a mocking smile and moved back a little, raising his wineglass again. "To Leoni," he said, "the most improbable matchmaker anyone could have."

"Yes, isn't she?" Callie agreed dryly, but then she laughed and lifted her own glass in a fond salute. "To Leoni."

They spoke of everything and nothing after that, content to let time and the world flow by as they sat in the window booth at Leoni's Café. Callie felt as if all of her senses had somehow shifted to a new, higher level. Maybe it was because of the wine she drank or perhaps it was Nick's company or even Leoni's heavy-handed matchmaking, but whatever it was, the night took on a feeling of enchantment. Dinner was no longer ordinary roast beef, but ambrosia; the wine not burgundy, but sweet nectar. The air around her was scented with the pungent aroma of the chrysanthemum she wore pinned at her breast, and in the soft candlelight, Nick's hair seemed to flash with blue fire, his eyes to soften to the color of a twilight sky.

Nick walked her home after that, through the cold winter night. "I don't think I've ever seen so many stars," he said, gazing up at the sky.

"Do you think you'll learn to like it here?" she asked as they stopped in front of her door.

He brought his gaze back to her. "It all depends...."

There it was again, that unspoken challenge in his words. And a part of her clamored to rise to it. But the common sense part of her still held sway. He was not the right man for her. "I'd better go in now," she said hurriedly, tamping down her wayward emotions. "Tomorrow is going to be a long day."

He gave her a wide smile, as if he sensed her dilemma and relished it. "Good night, Callie."

She mustered a slight smile in return. "Good night, Nick."

He turned to leave and then paused. "Oh, what the hell," he muttered to himself and turned back to her. "I think Leoni just might have succeeded this time." Without another word, he took her into his arms and kissed her until she was breathless, until the stars in the sky began to whirl and fall, until she was consumed by the raging inferno inside of her.

By midmorning the next day, the store and everything in it was covered with plaster dust. Callie sneezed, sneezed again and wiped an arm over her streaming eyes. Nick had explained to her that all the old walls had to be ripped out before they could put the new walls up, but he hadn't told her how dusty the whole process would be. Using the claw end of a large hammer, they tore out the walls, sending large chunks of plaster crashing to the floor and large clouds of dust billowing into the air.

She glanced over at him now and felt that odd weak-in-the-knees breathlessness from the night before seize her again. After he'd kissed her, he'd left her without more than a gruff "you'd better go inside now, Caledonia." And now this morning he'd been, if not exactly glacial in his attitude toward her, decidedly cool. It was as if they'd entered into a tacit agreement to ignore what had happened between them.

But she couldn't ignore it. He'd kissed her like...like what? She attacked the old wall with renewed vigor as she tried to decide. He'd kissed her, she thought slowly, like he had the right to. As if he had some claim to her.

Well, circumstances might have given him some sort of professional hold on her, she thought with a blaze of righteous indignation, but it did not extend to her personal life.

And then like an errant breeze on a hot summer day came the memory of his kiss, and her mouth softened in remembrance. He'd been so beautiful standing there in the moonlight, with his midnight hair and his forget-me-not eyes. And when he'd pressed his mouth on hers, gently at first then with growing urgency, her lips had parted and welcomed him....

"Callie?"

"Nick." She sighed, seeing him through the mists of last night's magic so that she wondered now how his hair had come to be covered with white plaster dust.

He took it all in without comment, from her memory-clouded eyes to her softly parted lips. Like the hawk he suddenly resembled, he seemed to miss very little. "Aunt Jessie just called down. She wants us to come up for tea."

Callie made a rapid readjustment to the present. "Your hair is all white."

"So's yours." He laughed. "You'll make quite a senior citizen."

She sneezed again. "If I live that long."

"Let's go get that tea and let the dust settle for a while."

They brushed themselves off and climbed the stairs to the tiny apartment on the second floor. Aunt Jessie and Shadow, with all six kittens in tow, met them at the door. "Come in, my dears. The tea is just about ready."

Callie sat down in the midst of the rollicking kittens. "Look, they've got their eyes open."

Aunt Jessie beamed proudly at her little brood. "Since yesterday."

Nick knelt beside Callie. "I'd like one," he said unexpectedly and scooped a dark gray kitten with four neat white paws into his arms.

Callie looked at him in fascination and a shiver of desire rippled through her. The tiny kitten cradled in his large hands presented such a vivid contrast, she had an unexpected vision of what it would be like to have his hands caress her in that same gentle way.

"I think Baker's should keep at least one of Shadow's progeny in residence even after Shadow is gone," she heard him say, and his words brought her thudding back to reality.

She scrambled to her feet and after mumbling something about washing up, made a dash for the kitchen. She hated being reminded that Aunt Jessie was moving to California. But the reminders, like keeping one of Shadow's kittens after Shadow was gone, were coming so fast and furious now, they couldn't be avoided.

She twisted the faucet on and let cold water rush over her wrists. She and Aunt Jessie had not really talked much about the impending move. Every time she brought it up, Aunt Jessie would pat her soothingly on the arm and in that maddening way she had of shielding her from any bad news, tell her not to worry about it. Well, she *was* worried. What if Aunt Jessie hated California? What if she and Maude simply could not get along?

"Callie, dear, do come for tea now."

Callie glanced over her shoulder and found her aunt hovering in the doorway. "Aunt Jessie, have you heard from Maude recently?"

"I don't want you to worry about Maude, dear. You have so many other things on your mind right now."

Callie was suddenly exasperated. "Aunt Jessie, please just tell me if you've heard anything further from Maude. The truth would make me worry less."

Aunt Jessie advanced into the kitchen and wrapped her niece in an unexpected hug. "I'm an old fool, aren't I? Of course you want to know what's going on. It's just hard for me to remember you're a grown-up woman now and not a little girl anymore."

"Everything's changing so fast. From Nick taking over the store to you leaving. I'm having trouble getting used to it, that's all."

"Things will turn out for the best, you'll see."

"I don't see how they can."

Aunt Jessie chuckled a little. "Neither do I," she confessed. "But I'm sure they will. Somehow. Maybe Maude will have a conversion experience, something like that old Ebenezer Scrooge did in *A Christmas Carol*, and turn into a warm, caring, kindhearted woman."

Callie and Aunt Jessie looked soberly at each other for a moment. "No way," they chorused in unison and then started to laugh.

"Aunt Jessie," Callie finally said, still chuckling, "if that boiled old owl gives you any trouble, you just send for me."

"I can handle Maude, don't you worry about it."

"How?"

"Just like I always have. I pretend I'm a rock and she's a trickle of water. I listen to her, agree to go along with whatever she says and then do things my way."

"But look what's happened. She's gotten her way in the end."

Aunt Jessie smiled. "It's taken that drip of water twenty years to wear away the rock, hasn't it?"

Callie had to laugh again. "I never thought of it that way."

"So, are you going to stop worrying about me?"

Callie shook her head. "No."

"I'm not going to stop worrying about you, either, so I guess we're even. And to answer your question, Maude wrote and said she'd be here in a week or so to help me pack up. Now I think we'd better go see to your young man. He might wonder what's become of us."

"Aunt Jessie, please. He's not my young man."

Aunt Jessie gave her a little wink. "No, of course not, dear."

Callie knew as she trailed her aunt into the next room that the rock trick was in full effect. Only this time it was being used against her.

## Chapter Five

The store was in shambles. Callie sat on an up-turned box and surveyed the mess in awed silence. It was hard to think that she and Nick had done all this in just a couple of days with only two hammers and a lot of sweat.

Nick sat beside her on another box, legs comfortably propped on yet a third. "This is always the point in a job when it looks hopeless."

It looked that all right. "What happens next?"

He grinned. "Clean up. How are you with a broom?"

"More experienced than with a hammer." She grimaced as she nursed a wounded finger. "This is turning out to be so much fun."

"Do I hear a note of sarcasm in your voice?"

"Who me, sarcastic?"

"Just a touch."

"Just a touch," she agreed with a laugh and then resolutely climbed to her feet. "I'll go get the brooms."

"Who said anything about brooms? I said, broom, singular."

Callie surveyed him through widely innocent eyes. "Why, Nick, how sweet of you to offer to clean this up by yourself."

"Make that brooms, plural," he said quickly and was rewarded with one of her rare, as of late, light-hearted peals of laughter.

"I'll be right back."

It took them what was left of the day to sweep the store clean of the worst of the plaster dust. But at last the job was done and Callie leaned gratefully on her broom, glad to have it over with.

"Are you hungry?" she asked Nick as he swept the last of the pile into a trash bag.

He paused and leaning on his own broom, gave her a wicked smile. "Why, Caledonia, are you asking me over to your place for dinner?"

She almost choked. She hadn't had that in mind at all. "I . . . that is, we . . ."

"Yes . . . ?" he prompted, the smile widening at her discomfiture.

There was no way she wanted him in the close confines of her small house. That might lead to . . . well, never mind. She wasn't going to let it happen. She had already decided—more than once—to keep him at arm's length. That would be a whole lot easier if she avoided being alone with him in an intimate setting like her home.

And then inspiration struck. "Why don't I run out for Chinese and bring it back here?"

His blue eyes sparkled with amusement. "That sounds great. I love picnics."

She gulped. Picnics brought to mind all sorts of romantic possibilities. But it seemed as if she had painted herself into an inescapable corner. "Be right back," she said, and leaning her broom against what was left of one wall, almost ran to get her coat.

She found when she walked back into the store a half an hour later that Nick had been hard at work while she'd been gone. He'd cleared the drop cloth off an old clawfooted table and had even arranged candles in a tarnished silver candelabrum on top of it.

Callie set her packages down on the table and surveyed his handiwork with trepidation, remembering where a little candlelight had led them once before. "I've never heard of candles at a picnic."

"Then you've never been on a picnic with me. It's standard."

This was not going well. "Why don't I run up and ask Aunt Jessie to join us?" Callie conceded that her aunt wasn't a very reliable duenna with all of her matchmaking instincts, but she would have to do.

Nick shook his head. "I just spoke to her. She's already eaten and is now, according to her, ready for bed."

"Oh." And then, "You can handle this, Callie," she muttered, knowing she had only her good intentions to rely upon.

"What's that?"

"Nothing," she said quickly. She pulled out a chair and sat down, briskly distributing the white cartons of food. "Let's eat. Everything's getting cold." They were going to have a no-nonsense dinner, and then she was going to go right home.

Nick sat down across from her and busied himself with the various little boxes. "This is good," he said through a mouthful of Mongolian beef. "You're a wonderful cook."

She grinned at him. "Thanks. I slaved over this all day."

"I have help in the kitchen, you know."

No, she hadn't known. This was an entirely new development. Maybe a girlfriend he hadn't bothered to mention before. "Who's that?" she asked with surprising asperity, sounding even to herself as if she were jealous.

He cocked an eyebrow at her, not continuing on until she began to shift uncomfortably under his far-too-penetrating look. "Oh, lots of people," he finally said, "Sara Lee, Chef Boyardee, Mrs. Paul."

She laughed, relief making her slightly giddy. "I know them."

"Small world," he observed, grinning.

"Very," she agreed, matching his smile.

"Let's drink to it." He toasted her with a cup of green tea.

They sipped their tea in companionable silence for a while, but then Nick stirred restlessly in his chair. "Would you like to hear some music?" he asked her.

She thought he was teasing again and decided to get into the spirit of the game early this time. "Gershwin would be nice, or Irving Berlin."

Unexpectedly, Nick set his tea down and got up from the table. "Be right back," he told her and disappeared into the shadowy depths of the store.

"Where are you going?" she called after him.

"You'll see," he answered faintly.

While Callie waited, she heard him give an indistinct sneeze and then a muffled shout of triumph. In a few moments he trotted back to her bearing a cardboard box full of old 78-rpm records. "Look through these," he told her, "while I find something to play them on."

Callie flipped through the old records, selecting one here and there until she had a stack of about a dozen. By that time, Nick was back with an old-fashioned gramophone complete with fluted horn. "Give me the first one," he said, cranking up the spring motor. She handed him Glenn Miller's 'In the Mood.' "Good choice," he said approvingly and set the record spinning on the turntable.

They sipped their tea while they listened to the scratchy rendition of the old song, both of them tapping their fingers to the beat of the big-band era. "Take the A Train" was next and then "Pennsylvania 6-5000."

"Would you put on 'Blue Moon'?" Callie asked. "It's one of my favorites."

Obligingly, Nick set the record on the gramophone and then taking the teacup from Callie's hand and setting it aside, he drew her to her feet. "May I have this dance, Miss Baker."

So much for good intentions, she thought, unable to resist either the music or him. "Why, certainly, Mr. Logan. But just this one and then it's time for me to go home."

Nick swept her into his arms and waltzed her around the store, stepping nimbly over boxes and around sheet-swathed furniture. "You dance divinely, Miss Baker," he murmured, waltzing her close to the table as the song came to an end. And then in a deft move, he cranked the motor again, set the needle at the start of the record and danced her off around the room.

"But . . ." Callie began to protest.

"If I remember correctly, Miss Baker, you said just this one and it is, still, just this one."

She had to laugh at being so skillfully outmaneuvered. "Okay," she conceded, "just until *the end* of this one."

Nick held her close, his hand warm and sure at her waist. Callie leaned her head against his chest and sighed. She could no more have resisted him than if she were a leaf born along on a swiftly running river.

"Having fun?" His deep voice rumbled under her cheek.

She lifted her head to look at him, at his imperious features that had somehow softened until she wondered why she'd ever thought them arrogant. "Wonderful fun."

For a long moment they looked into each other's eyes, and some strong, elemental emotion passed between them. Callie knew she couldn't look away, and knew on a much deeper level, that she didn't want to. His eyes still locked on hers, Nick lowered his head and caught her lips with his own.

Callie knew that somewhere the scratchy music played on, knew in fact that she must still be breathing, but with that kiss her world seemed to stop. As her lips clung to his, she moved her hands to the midnight satin of his hair and tangled them in its silken softness.

He crushed her even closer and deepened the kiss, exploring the edges of her mouth with his tongue, until with a small cry of pleasure, Callie gave herself over to the exquisite sensations.

Neither of them heard the key turn in the front door nor felt the icy gust of wind that swirled into the store and sent the candles on the table into a wild, flickering dance of their own. They were oblivious to the heavy footsteps that crossed the floor to where they stood or to the black eyes that surveyed them with glittering shrewdness. "Is this what I'm paying you all that money for, Mr. Logan?" a voice rasped over the haunting melody of "Blue Moon," "to seduce my great-niece?"

Callie pulled away from Nick as if she'd been shot. "Aunt Maude!" she gasped, the blood draining from her face. "What are you doing here?"

"Checking up on things, and none too soon, I see."

Nick's mouth lifted in a sardonic smile. "Miss Baker," he murmured, his voice cool and utterly unapologetic, "what a pleasant surprise."

Maude Baker shouted with laughter. "I'll just bet it is. Now, let go of my niece. I want her to take me up to Jessie's place. I've been traveling for most of the day and I'm tired."

Nick's arm tightened around her, and Callie thought for one heart-stopping moment he was going to refuse. She knew he despised preemptory orders of any kind. In that regard they were alike. But this was no time for a showdown. "I'll bring your bags up," he finally said, and with a sigh of relief, Callie slipped from his arms.

Maude directed Nick out to a waiting cab and then turned to Callie. "Don't just stand there girl. Take me upstairs."

Callie's resentment of her aunt's imperious ways flared into actual dislike. But she didn't want to antagonize her with a richly deserved piece of her mind. They would all be made to pay the price. "We weren't expecting you this soon," she said instead, keeping her voice carefully neutral.

"I like to arrive earlier than expected. You never know what you might turn up." The piercing look she gave Callie said all the rest.

They reached the upstairs apartment and found Aunt Jessie hovering in the doorway. "I thought I heard you, Maude. Come in. I've only just now baked some of your favorite cookies. You know, the white ones, dipped in powdered sugar.''

Maude made a noise that was half grunt of disapproval and half groan of anticipation. "I'm too fat as it is, but I'll take one." Jessie motioned her sister into the dining room and then bustled off for the cookies.

Maude leveled her piercing black eyes on Callie. "Well, young lady, what exactly was going on down there?''

Callie was not going to be intimidated by Maude. The Baker self-assurance ran in her blood, too. "I was kissing Nick Logan."

"I could see that," Maude said caustically. "Have you gone and fallen in love with the man?"

"No," she said tersely. It was on her lips to tell her aunt it was none of her business whether she was in love with Nick or not, but the older woman's next words stopped her in her tracks.

"Good. I won't have to fire one of you then."

Callie was incredulous. "Fire one of us? Which one?"

Maude gave Callie a tight-lipped smile. "Who do you think?"

Callie knew Maude wouldn't fire her. After all, they were family. "Nick," she barely breathed, and saw her aunt's almost imperceptible nod of agreement.

Here it is, she thought, what she'd wanted from the very start, to have Nick replaced. All she had to do was say she loved him. The situation was so ironic she almost wanted to laugh—or cry. But one thing she knew for certain; no matter how much she wanted Baker's, she wouldn't hurt Nick to get it. The knowledge was a revelation in itself.

"Well, Caledonia, do I have your promise that your little affair is at an end?"

Slowly Callie nodded, not bothering to correct her aunt's mistaken assumption that she and Nick had carried their relationship beyond the kissing stage. She had already decided they should keep their relationship on a completely professional level. In fact, had decided it several times, although circumstances and a pair of incredibly blue eyes kept getting in the way of her resolve. Maude's ultimatum only added weight to her decision.

"I warn you," Maude said, "I will not have any more hanky-panky going on in my store. I need one hundred percent of your energy directed at saving this business. If I find out that you have continued your affair with Mr. Logan even after this warning, he will be dismissed. Do I make myself clear?"

"Yes," Callie finally said, although she felt her heart give a rebellious twist.

Maude smiled with satisfaction. "I knew you had a level head under all that wild red hair of yours."

Aunt Jessie reappeared then and stopped Callie's sharp retort. "Here are the cookies," she warbled, and set them down with a flourish.

Maude took one and bit into it eagerly. "When you move in with me, you'll do all the cooking, of course."

Jessie gave Callie an almost imperceptible smile. "Of course," she answered sweetly, and even through her pain, Callie almost laughed out loud. Somehow Aunt Jessie would contrive to get out of it, either by cooking inedible dishes or ones that Maude disliked.

They heard Nick thumping up the stairs then, and Callie quickly opened the door for him. Bowed under the weight of three large suitcases, he managed to edge his way through the door before dropping them.

"Maude," Jessie asked, eyeing the mountain of luggage, "how long are you planning to stay?"

Maude cast a grim eye around the cluttered apartment. "One week. With a lot of hard work, we should be able to get your things in order by then."

Only one week and Aunt Jessie would be gone? The thought made Callie want to cry. Sensing his eyes on her, she glanced over at Nick, and while he looked sympathetic, she knew she could seek no comfort there. The strength she would need to get through the next days and weeks would have to come from within herself.

Suddenly weary beyond bearing, Callie got to her feet and announced her intention to go back to her apartment. "I'm tired," she explained to her aunts. "It's been a long day."

Nick, too, rose to his feet. "I'll see you home, Callie."

Maude glared at him. "Sit down, young man, I'm not through with you. I have a few things I want to get off my chest."

The atmosphere grew tense as Nick battled for self-control. "I'll be back in fifteen minutes and you can chew on me all you want," he finally said, voice implacable. "But right now, I'm seeing Callie home."

"Please, Nick," Callie said, suddenly alarmed for him, "it's all right." She was quite sure Aunt Maude would carry out her threat if she felt Callie wasn't living up to her part of the bargain. "I can see myself home. After all, I've been doing it for years."

"Are you sure?" he asked and received a loud grunt of disapproval from Maude.

Callie's brown eyes held a mute appeal for understanding. "Stay here, please."

He hesitated for a long moment and then reluctantly gave in with a slight shrug. "Sleep well, Callie."

She knew she wouldn't sleep at all but she didn't say so. "Good night everyone," she murmured, and then hurried out the door before she did something completely humiliating, like cry.

Maude waited until Callie was gone and Jessie had disappeared into the kitchen before she again barked an order for Nick to sit down. "Mr. Logan, I can tell that you have developed a certain affection for my niece. But you are running a store here, not a dating service. If you cannot resist temptation, I will be forced to remove it."

Nick's mouth tightened, but he didn't deny the accusation. "Meaning?"

"Just what I said. I have hired you to turn this store around. If I must, I will fire Caledonia so that you can get on with the business at hand."

Anger pulled Nick's face into a dark scowl. "Then I resign," he stated flatly.

Maude shrugged. "As you will. But then I will shut Baker's down and both you and that chit of girl will be out of job."

"But Callie loves this store." The words exploded from him.

Maude shrugged again. "That can't be helped."

Nick struggled silently with the alternatives. And then his shoulders sagged with sudden defeat. "I'll stay away from her," he said tonelessly.

"I knew when you understood the situation, your head would rule your heart. Now, I'm going to bed. As my niece said, it's been a long day. I trust I will see you at the store early tomorrow morning."

Mouth grim, Nick nodded his compliance.

Callie thought she would have to treat Nick with cool indifference in order to keep him at arm's length. But when she got to the store the next day, he was already hard at work and paused only long enough to give her some curt instructions before putting the entire length of the store between them.

Her job was to nail the new switch and electrical outlet boxes in place around the store. It required only a minimum amount of concentration so her mind was free to wander. After last night, she'd thought she would be the one to have to distance herself from him. But the opposite was true. He was more remote today than she'd ever seen him.

When she'd nailed the last box in place, she went in search of him, finding him hunched over the desk, hard at work on his scale drawing again. "I'm all done," she told his back.

He didn't turn around. "Good."

"Don't you want to take a look and see if everything is in order?"

He still refused to turn around. "You're a very competent woman, Callie. I'm sure everything is fine."

Had Maude said something to him, after all, to cause him to be so brusque? No, she decided, Nick Logan would quit rather than have his life manipulated by anyone. She knew him well enough by now to be sure of that. He was probably just in a bad mood. "What are you working on?" she asked pleasantly, and leaned over his shoulder to see what was so interesting. As she did so, a long tendril of her hair brushed across his face.

He sat unmoving for a moment, his eyes squeezed shut as if he were in pain. "Dammit, Callie," he finally said, angrily brushing her hair away. "Can't you see I'm busy here?"

She backed off, but her own quick temper surfaced. "All I did was ask you a simple question."

"Okay, look." With another harsh oath, he pushed away from the desk, giving her ample opportunity to see the drawing without any possibility of touching him again. "The light fixtures you selected are out of stock until June. The lighting company called me this morning about it. I've gone ahead and sketched in something else."

"But this is track lighting," she protested. "I thought we decided not to go that way."

"You decided," he ground out. "I still think this is the best alternative."

She couldn't believe what she was hearing. "What about my opinion? I thought this was a joint project."

He was so angry now, he was shouting. "I have final say on all decisions."

"But this is wrong," she cried.

"Look, Callie, you're going to have to learn to take orders if you want to work with me."

He had turned into a bully, an insufferable, pigheaded bully. "Then maybe I don't want to work with you. This isn't the army and you're not my sergeant."

"Fine."

"Fine!" she shouted back, and they glared at each other in tight-lipped fury.

Callie cooled off suddenly. They weren't going to get anywhere shouting at each other. "Let me go back to the lighting store and see what other alternatives are available," she said, appealing to his sense of reason.

He glared at her a moment longer and then his features relaxed. "Okay. But keep it within the budget and this time, make sure they can deliver within the next two weeks."

"Right," she said, and gave him a tentative smile, hoping for a truce.

His expression grew bleak. "Go now, Callie, before I say or do something I may regret."

She turned and stumbled away. What had happened between last night and today to make him treat her like this? After all, she was the one who was protecting him from Maude's wrath, not the opposite. His attitude could only mean one thing. She had only been a diversion to him and now the boss was here, playtime was over. The realization hurt—hurt so deeply it surprised her.

"I don't have to do it," she mumbled to herself as she shrugged into her coat and made her way out of the store. "I can get him fired tomorrow if I want to. All I have to do is kiss him again." And then she laughed. She was no Jezebel to use her feminine wiles against him. And judging from what had just happened, there was little chance of that. He probably wouldn't let her get within ten feet of him again anyway.

Picking out new lighting fixtures turned out to be just what she needed to put her pain and anger aside. She spent several hours happily looking at everything from crystal chandeliers to paddle fans, so absorbed by her task that her troubles faded into the back of her mind. Finally, she settled on a Tiffany style that was sleek enough to suit Nick and yet elegant enough to please her. After several assurances that the lights would be available when they needed them, Callie headed for home.

She found Nick where she had left him, still hard at work over his scale drawing. "Mission accomplished," she announced, perching on one corner of the desk.

Nick seemed to have gotten over his earlier mood. He leaned back in his chair and gave her one of his old, heart-winning smiles. "I take it you found something to your liking."

"And yours, too," she assured him. "The fixtures are in a Tiffany style, but made mainly of clear glass so they have a contemporary feel."

"And the delivery?"

"Set for two weeks, just like you wanted."

"Good."

She looked at him thoughtfully for a moment. "Nick, about this morning. . . ." she began.

"Forget it."

"No, I can't, not until we clear the air. I'm sorry I overreacted." If he wanted a strictly businesslike relationship, she would give it to him.

"It's understandable," he said. "I came across like a real jerk."

"Well. . . ." she said.

He tore at her heart with his easy laugh. "You're not supposed to agree with me."

"Let's just say we both responded a little more strongly than we should have."

"No overstatement there."

"Why don't we agree to peacefully disagree next time?"

"Do you think there will be a next time?"

It was her turn to laugh. "Absolutely. Do we have a deal?" She thrust out her hand.

"Deal."

As soon as Nick took her hand, she realized her mistake. A fierce longing for him swept through her, leaving her shaken with its intensity. It was then she knew she no longer wanted him out of the store and out of her life. Somehow, this impossible man had gotten into her blood. "Nick," she said, her voice barely a whisper.

It was as if he, too, were in the grip of some strong emotion, for his face seemed to mirror her own longing. "Ah, Callie, what's going to come of all this?"

Before she could think of anything to say, she heard the overhead apartment door creak open and footsteps begin their slow, heavy descent. "Maude," Callie gasped, and wasn't sure whether she snatched her hand away first or if he did.

That same implacable look from earlier settled over Nick's face. "Get away from here," he ordered.

"Gladly," she snapped back, and stalked away, reminded again that the store was far more important to him than she was.

By the time Maude reached the bottom step, Callie had put half the store between herself and Nick. Keeping her back firmly turned on him, she still managed to hear his conversation with Maude.

"Well, young man, how are things coming?"

Nick was still angry and it showed. "It's slow," he snapped.

"Any personal reasons for that?" If Callie had turned around, she would have found her aunt's black eyes trained on her.

"No," Nick said, his voice losing some of it's angry quality. "None."

Maude nodded. "Good. Now, show me around the store. I want to see what you've done so far. Callie," she called, "I want you to come with us."

The last thing Callie wanted was to spend any time with either Aunt Maude or Nick. But there was no graceful way out of it, so she trailed along behind them while Nick explained what they had done and what still lay ahead. "First new walls, then wiring, a new ceiling and light fixtures, paint and wallpaper and finally new carpet."

If Maude approved, she gave little indication beyond, "How long will all of this take?"

"We should be ready to open up in another month."

"Jessie and I will come back for the grand opening."

Callie hated the way Maude had assumed control over Aunt Jessie's life. "I'm going to give a farewell party for Aunt Jessie," she said suddenly, and when Maude leveled one of her black stares on her, Callie dared her to say no with a long look of her own.

At last Maude gave a mirthless laugh. "You're a Baker all right. Give your party, Caledonia. It's fine with me."

Callie hadn't been asking for Maude's permission. She'd give a party for Aunt Jessie if she wanted to. But it was better not to say so. No use antagonizing Aunt Maude needlessly. "Next Saturday," she said instead, "here in the store. We'll just clear away the mess and set some tables out."

Unexpectedly, Nick gave her a thumbs-up sign over Maude's head. And then, even more unexpectedly, he winked.

Callie was warmed by his surprising show of approval. But as she went about making her plans, she couldn't decide if it was for the party or her willingness to defy her aunt.

## Chapter Six

Bright pink streamers and multicolored helium balloons festooned the store, lending the new but completely bare walls a festive look. Arms sore from tacking up at least ten miles of crepe paper, Callie paused in her decorating and looked down at the store from her vantage point on a tall stepladder. There were still a million details to take care of before the party that night, but she had to admit things were coming along nicely.

With Nick's help she had cleared a space in the center of the store and set out chairs and tables for the guests. The old gramophone and a stack of 78s would provide the music, Leoni the food and Nick the entertainment.

Callie glanced down at him now and wondered what exactly it was he was planning. He'd announced his intentions two days earlier, saying only that he'd take care of that part of the evening's festivities, and then proceeded to give her a mysterious smile every time she'd begged him for more information. Other than those smiles, he'd maintained his remote attitude toward her during all of their work together.

She should have been glad. It made things easier for her. She didn't have to come up with a dozen different excuses for keeping her distance. But the funny thing was, his attitude hurt more than it helped. She wanted to feel that by staying away from him she was being noble. Instead she felt confused.

Her feelings for him had undergone a remarkable change over the past few weeks. She'd always found him attractive. She was no more immune to a handsome man than any other woman. But at first she hadn't liked him very well. In fact, she'd all but hated him.

But now? Now, all of that had changed. She had some decidedly tender feelings for him even if he didn't reciprocate them.

"All done?" he asked, catching her look.

"Almost. How about you?"

He deftly filled another balloon with helium and sent it bobbing in her direction. She swiped at it, missed and then laughed as the balloon made a bid for freedom in the shadowy rafters of the store. "You've lost more than you've hung on to," she teased, counting at least ten balloons on the ceiling.

"Why don't you come down here and see if you can do any better."

This was the first time in almost a week he'd given into the easy banter Maude's appearance had ended so abruptly. "I just might do that," she said, and started down the ladder, called by his teasing smile, hurrying when she knew she shouldn't. But in her haste, she missed a step, grabbed for the ladder and fell backward, landing in a crumpled heap on the floor.

"Callie!" Nick cried, rushing to her side.

Her face was white with pain. "Oh, Nick, I think I hurt my foot."

He scooped her into his arms and lifted her easily from the floor, holding her tight against his chest. "Idiot," he crooned, "don't you know you're not supposed to do stunt dives off a ladder?"

She managed a laugh. "I'll try to remember that next time."

"I suppose I ought to set you down someplace and see about your foot," he murmured, but made no move to find a chair, instead holding her even tighter against his chest, face buried in the softness of her hair.

Callie's arms crept around his neck. "You don't want to strain your back," she sighed, leaning her head against his chest, the pain in her foot as well as the reason she was supposed to stay away from him completely forgotten.

"No," he agreed.

"You'd better put me down then," she said, although it was the last thing on earth she wanted.

She heard the front door open and Nick, who had a clear view of whomever it was who had entered the store, hastily placed her on a nearby chair. "Show me where your foot hurts," he commanded roughly, his voice unnaturally loud.

Puzzled at the swift change in his attitude, Callie looked over her shoulder and, heart sinking, saw both Maude and Leoni standing just inside the door. Of all the rotten luck, it had to be the improbable combination of those two to catch them together. "Aunt Maude, Leoni!" Callie said, hoping her voice didn't betray any of the nervous guilt she was feeling. "I've hurt my foot."

"I can see that," Maude snapped, and with Leoni right behind her, walked over and bent to take a closer look.

Leoni glanced from Nick to Callie, a ribald smile curving her mouth. "I used to say I had something in my eye." She elbowed Callie's shoulder. "It worked better, honey. Got the young man headed in the right direction at least." And then she peered at Callie's foot for the first time. "Why, your ankle actually does look swollen," she said, obviously surprised.

"Can you imagine that," Maude added sarcastically.

Nick's face showed his irritation. "Does it still hurt, Callie?" he asked, ignoring the gibes from their audience.

She tried wiggling her foot. "A little," she admitted, although it hurt more than that.

He carefully laid her foot down. "Maybe you should see the doctor."

"Maybe," Maude said, breaking in, "you should call off this party. With your foot like that, how can you entertain?"

Nick smiled at Callie. "Oh, I'm taking care of the entertainment."

Even with Maude's dour presence looming over her, Callie couldn't help but tease him. "You're doing card tricks, aren't you?"

"Nope," he grinned.

"Magic?"

"No."

"What then?"

"You'll just have to wait and see."

"What is all this about?" Maude demanded.

"For heaven's sake, Maude," Leoni bellowed in her best waitress-intimidating voice, "let these young people alone. Can't you see they're not interested in you."

"Or in anything else," Maude muttered grimly.

Leoni was more than a match for Maude. "You just hate it when you're not queen bee, that's all. Now come along. With Callie hurt, you're going to have to pitch in and help with the party."

"I want no part of it. None of this falderal was my idea," Maude protested.

"And that's the only reason you don't like it," Leoni said, and sniffed. "Callie, child, is Jessie upstairs? Good. We'll just go on up there and make a few plans of our own while your young man tends to your foot—and other things," she added, mercifully keeping her usual leer down to a raised eyebrow and a bawdy wink.

After the two women had gone, Callie and Nick exchanged smiles. "I'm not sure which one of them is worse," she said.

"I think I'd prefer to have both of them find something else to focus on," he answered, vexation back in his voice, and then he switched subjects. "Are you sure you don't want to see a doctor?"

She shook her head. The pain was already subsiding.

"Then you should put some ice on your foot before it really starts to swell. I'll just run upstairs and get some from Aunt Jessie."

She watched him go and then shifted impatiently in her chair, thinking of all she had left to do before the party. After a particularly sharp pang in her foot, she realized with a resigned sigh that she wasn't going to be the one to get it done. She would have to leave it all up to her aunts, Leoni and Nick.

Nick. This afternoon he'd gone from remote to friendly to romantic and back to aloof in all of about five minutes. There was just no figuring him out. It was almost, she thought again, as if Aunt Maude had had her little talk with him instead of her. But that was impossible. Nick would never stand for Maude's interference. If she threatened him with his job, he'd quit. Callie was certain of it.

So what was the answer? She shook her head. There didn't seem to be one.

"Who are you arguing with?" Nick asked with that disconcerting knack he had of reading her thoughts.

Callie looked up and saw him, ice bag in hand, standing by her chair. "Myself," she admitted, wondering if he could also detect the nature of her argument.

But if he could, he didn't give any indication of it. Instead, he leaned over her foot and gently applied the ice bag. "You'll have to keep off of this," he advised, examining an already visible bruise.

"Maybe we should call off the party."

"Not on your life. Those three women are in heaven up there, organizing this thing. It would break their hearts to have it canceled."

"I can't believe Maude is helping."

"Believe it," he said, his own surprise showing. "She and Leoni are fighting for the job of chief while Aunt Jessie seems content to play Indian."

That sounded just about par for the course. "Maybe I should go home then, and give myself plenty of time to get ready."

He gave her that lazy grin of his. "You want me to carry you there?"

And have Maude catch them? Not a prayer, although the idea of being scooped into his strong arms again and held against his broad chest was an intriguing one. "I think I can hobble out to my car and drive home."

"Why don't I pick you up about seven and bring you back?"

"I'd like that." She stood up and gingerly tested her injured foot. "Beyond a twinge or two, I think I'm okay," she announced and, with a small wave, limped off.

Nick's eyes followed her until she was out the door. "You, Caledonia Baker," he said to the empty store, "are much, much more than okay." Whistling a few bars of "Blue Moon," he turned then, filled up another helium balloon and sent it winging to the ceiling.

Foot wrapped in several elastic bandages and propped on a small stool, Callie sat amidst the noise and hubbub of the party, enjoying herself immensely. All of Aunt Jessie's friends from Sassafras Street had turned out for the affair, intent upon giving her a truly memorable send-off. Callie searched the crowd for her aunt and found her, flushed and excited, chatting with Ralph Donaldson and his wife, Mamie, from the dry-goods store.

Nick made his way through the crowd and took the chair next to her, handing her a glass of wine. "Having fun?"

She smiled. "I thought you could tell those things just by looking at me."

"Let me see if that's true," he said, and cupped her chin in his hand. He studied her face for a long moment, eyes so intimate, she felt as if he'd actually wrapped her in his arms. "You're having fun," he affirmed. "You love a party. But what's this I see? Sorrow mixed in with the happiness?"

"Because Aunt Jessie is leaving."

He grinned and let his hand fall away. "So's Aunt Maude."

"That's true," she agreed, laughing, and then shook her head. "I don't know how Aunt Jessie is going to manage her."

"Even as heavy-handed as Maude is about it, I think your aunts would really like to improve their relationship. But they're going to have to work it out for themselves."

Callie was doubtful. "Do you think they can?"

"It's going to take quite a bit of compromise on both their parts, but, yes, I do."

"It's interesting you should say that when compromise doesn't come very naturally to you," she teased.

He feigned a wounded look. "How can you say that?"

"In case you've forgotten, we almost came to blows over whether the store should be pink or blue."

"I seem to remember someone else having trouble compromising."

"Who, me?"

He tugged at her hair. "Yes, you."

"So, Mr. Logan, you seem to have the answers to the mysteries of the universe tonight. What else do you recommend for a happy relationship?"

"Love, of course," he answered, and his eyes once more came to rest expectantly on her face.

She grew serious. "Are you saying that love conquers all?"

"Is that what you think?" he countered, eyes still intent on her face.

They seemed to be carrying on their conversation on two different levels. On the face of it, they were talking about Maude and Jessie. But it ran deeper than that, too, and so she answered carefully. "I'd like to think so...."

"But..." he prompted.

"But I think love takes a lot of hard work, patience and sacrifice."

"How about compromise?" he asked, the teasing back in his voice.

"All right, compromise," she conceded, laughing.

"It's taken your aunts a long time to realize it, and maybe they wouldn't be able to put words to it, but that's exactly what they're doing." He set his wine-glass aside and stood up. "Enough philosophizing. Time for my act. I think I need to liven up this party."

She was overwhelmed with curiosity. "What are you going to do?"

He shook his head at her. "Secrets drive you crazy, don't they, Callie?"

She turned laughing eyes up at him. "Only when I don't know what they are."

"Then it's time to put you out of your misery." He clapped his hands loudly. "Ladies and gentlemen," he called, "may I have your attention please. If you'll all help yourselves to another drink or a bite to eat and find a comfortable place to sit, the entertainment for this evening will begin." He looked down at her. "I'll see you afterward," he promised, and ambled away.

As she watched him go, her newly discovered feelings for him welled up inside of her again. He was still bossy and maddeningly arrogant, but he was so many other things, too, things she was finding all too fascinating for her—and his—own good.

Aunt Jessie settled on the chair Nick had just vacated and interrupted her musings. "My dear, this is the most delightful party. Thank you."

Callie patted her lovingly on the cheek. "I'm glad you're having a good time, Aunt Jessie. I'm just sorry you have to work at your own party."

"But I'm enjoying that, too. Maude and Leoni decided I should pass the hors d'oeuvres, so you see, I have the chance to get around to everyone."

Callie reached out and gave her aunt a hug. "Aunt Jessie, I do believe you're going to be all right in California. You seem to be able to find the good in every situation."

"Of course I do, dear. It's all a part of being a rock."

"I'm afraid I could never take life so stoically."

"You're too much like Maude, that's why," Jessie told her confidentially.

"I'm not like her," Callie denied, stung.

"Why, yes you are, dear. Not completely, of course. But you have some of the same stubbornness, temper, arrogance...."

Callie held up her hand. "Stop, please, Aunt Jessie. I'm not stubborn ... I'm determined. As for my temper, I'll admit it's quick, but only when somebody does something stupid." She realized what she'd just said and stopped. "Well, maybe I can be a touch arrogant," she conceded sheepishly.

"Yes, dear, you can. But then, can't we all? It's only human nature. But you are so many other wonderful things, too. As is Maude. You're both intelligent, honest, loyal and attractive—yes, Maude was quite pretty in her day. I think your young man appreciates all of those qualities."

Callie's train of thought shifted. She knew she had to discourage Aunt Jessie from thinking of Nick in that light. "He's not my young man, Aunt Jessie," she said earnestly.

The other woman laughed gaily. "The way you two look at each other, you would never know it."

Had all those tender feelings for him crept into her face? She'd have to be more careful in the future. "You have to believe me, Aunt Jessie. Nothing is going on between us."

"Oh, I know, dear. Maude takes great satisfaction in that. But if there's one thing I want you to remember, it's this. 'To thine ownself be true.'" Aunt Jessie leaned closer to her. "In other words, follow your heart, Callie, dear, and do what it tells you to do."

"But what about you? Aren't you letting Maude stampede you into something you don't want?"

Aunt Jessie shook her head. "Of course not. If I truly didn't want to go to California, I wouldn't. But I told you a while back that it was time to mend some fences. I've let the differences between us run on too long."

"I just wish you wouldn't let Maude think she's calling all the shots. It galls me to see her gloat."

"I'm becoming a diplomat in my old age, my dear. If it makes her happy to think that and doesn't compromise me, what is the harm?" Aunt Jessie sighed and then leaned closer to Callie again to whisper conspiratorially, "I think you and your young man might take a lesson from me."

"What do you mean?"

"Just this, don't wait until you're as old as I am to figure it all out. Love is much too precious to be ignored."

How ironic that both Nick and Aunt Jessie had chosen the same night to lecture her on the nature of love!

A stir in the crowd caught Callie's eye and she turned her attention toward it. It was then she saw Nick. He'd changed from his khaki slacks and plaid shirt into a tuxedo of questionable origins. Black with sequin-studded lapels, it came equipped with a red bow tie and cummerbund. But it was his top hat that really fascinated Callie. It was covered with dozens of multicolored flashing lights.

"Oh, Nick, bravo," she called, applauding loudly.

He looked toward her and with a flourish doffed the unusual hat and then held up his hands for quiet. "Ladies and gentlemen," he called, "I will now amaze and entertain you with that legendary instrument of fun, that delight of small boys, that joy of the school yard and bane of all teachers, the yo-yo." He pulled a bright red yo-yo from his pocket and sent it whirling toward the floor. "Perhaps a little history of the yo-yo will help you to understand its significance to the world. But first some musical accompaniment from my assistant, Mr. Paul Grogan. Mr. Grogan, if you please."

Leoni's chef stepped out of the crowd, bowed once and raised his harmonica to his mouth. "'Oh, Susanna,'" Nick announced, and the chef launched into his one and only song.

Callie laughed so hard, her sides ached. "This is wonderful," she managed to gasp to Aunt Jessie.

"There's more, dear," her aunt murmured, giving her a sideways glance that was an equal mixture of disapproval and perplexity.

Callie knew she could never explain why the harmonica music was so hysterically funny. "Do you think Nick really can yo-yo?"

"I do believe so, yes," Aunt Jessie answered. "He's been practicing upstairs."

"And you never told me?"

"I was sworn to secrecy, my dear. Now hush, I want to see this."

Callie turned her attention back to Nick. He let the yo-yo fly and started his patter again. "This trick is called Around the Corner, and that's where you'll find the yo-yo, around the corner." He worked the yo-yo around his back and gave a quick jerk on the string, spinning the yo-yo over his shoulder and into his hand. "And Around the World." He launched the yo-yo out in front of him and quickly rotated it over his head.

Amidst whistles and applause, Nick took a slight bow and resumed his speech, all the while performing tricks with the yo-yo. ''Some believe the Greeks invented the yo-yo twenty-five hundred years ago. It was popular in China, the Philippines and the courts of Europe. But nobody made it more popular than the all-American schoolboy.'' He paused, did a trick called the Forward Pass, acknowledged Callie with a nod and added, ''and schoolgirl, of course.

''Since we were all once denizens of the school yard, we all, more than likely, learned to yo. Who doesn't remember that thrill of triumph when he first learned to Walk the Dog.'' The yo-yo whirled to the ground and stayed there, spinning while Nick bounced it along the floor, taking it for a walk.

''With luck and practice, you next mastered the Three-Leaf Clover.'' The yo-yo flew over his head, out in front of him and then finally at knee level before snapping back into his hand again. ''You could Rock the Baby,'' he went on, quickly forming a triangle of string and gently rocking the whirling yo-yo in its center. ''Or a variation of the same, called Man on the Flying Trapeze.'' And here the yo-yo performed a feat of mind-boggling derring-do that had the crowd roaring its approval.

Nick signaled to Paul, the musical chef, that the finale was near, and the strains of ''Oh, Susanna'' grew louder. ''But the pièce de résistance in any school yard repertoire worth talking about has always been the Rocket.'' In a flash the red yo-yo disappeared and Nick produced a whirling orb that was lit from the inside with twinkling lights. "Ladies and Gentlemen, your complete attention, please."

Callie fastened her eyes on Nick and found to her surprise that she was holding her breath. How could he possibly top himself?

The glittering yo-yo flew straight up in the air and paused, for what seemed like forever, at the top of its arc. With a deft move, Nick slipped the string from his finger, gave it a sudden jerk, opened up his coat pocket and the yo-yo shot straight into it.

The applause was thunderous, and there were numerous cries for an encore, but Nick merely took a bow and turned to thank Paul for his dogged musical accompaniment.

Callie clapped until her hands ached and then clapped some more. She wanted to run to Nick to tell him how wonderful he'd been and cursed the injured foot that kept her immobile in her chair. "He's wonderful, isn't he, Aunt Jessie?" she said instead, her voice unknowingly full of pride.

Her aunt studied her face for a moment. "I wasn't sure if you realized that or not," she finally said.

Callie knew where the conversation was headed and didn't want it to go there. "I'm talking about the yo-yo."

"Well, I'm not. He's quite a catch."

"I'm not fishing."

"Oh, pish-tosh, Caledonia. If you're not, you should be."

"Should be what?" Nick asked, overhearing the last of this as he sat down next to Callie.

Callie gave her aunt a warning glance. She was growing tired of having her relationship with Nick pushed and pulled from one direction to the next by her interfering aunts. "You were sensational," she said, turning to him. "Where did you ever learn to do that?"

He gave her one of his wide-open smiles. "Do what?"

She hit him playfully on the arm. "Yo-yo."

"Around."

"Really, Nick."

"Really, Callie."

"No, I mean it. Did you go to school?"

He laughed. "That's right, the U. of Yo."

She laughed, too, and gave up. He obviously would rather tease her than tell her. "I love your tux," she said instead, "and especially the lights on your hat."

He flicked the brim of his hat. "Why, thank you, ma'am. It's all the rage, you know."

"Where?"

"Wherever I am."

"Nick, you're getting very close to unbearable."

"But you love me, right?"

Aunt Jessie gave a small chuckle. "Answer the man, Caledonia."

Callie groaned. "If I had two good feet I'd walk away from both of you."

"Where do you want to go?" Nick asked, his eyes gleaming with a wicked light.

"Anywhere. To the buffet table, I don't care."

Without another word, he scooped her into his arms and over her protests, strode to the buffet table. "What would you like?" he asked, studying the various dishes.

They made quite a sight with him in his madly twinkling hat and her with her hugely bandaged foot jutting out at such an odd angle from beneath her dress, and suddenly Callie laughed. She knew she should make him put her down but this was all just too crazy—and too fun—to resist. "I'd love a deviled egg, one of those chicken wings and a piece of lemon meringue pie."

He raised an eyebrow at her. "That's an interesting assortment."

She reached down and plucked one of the deviled eggs from the table. "Try this and then tell me if you could resist it." She held it up to his lips, and he ate it all, finally licking the last traces of it off her hand. Callie caught her breath as he gently sucked on her fingers, and she knew that not even a kiss could have been more intimate.

Unbidden, Aunt Maude came to mind, and Callie hastily pulled her hand away. "I—I think you should put me down now," she told him, still breathless. "I wouldn't want anyone to get the wrong impression." Especially Maude, she added silently.

"What impression would that be, Caledonia?" he asked softly without making a move to let her go.

She felt suddenly, irrationally, that she was a bone caught in the midst of a pack of dogs. But she knew what her duty was and she would do it regardless of how she was pushed and pulled in so many other directions. "Put me down," she insisted.

She saw his mouth tighten and thought he was going to say something harsh. But then he laughed, hugged her briefly and set her in a nearby chair. "You're a stubborn woman, Callie." He lifted his hat and ran his hand through his hair in a gesture of frustration. "That's one of the things I find so attractive about you. But for the life of me, I couldn't say why." He patted the hat back in place and without another word, left her to her own devices.

Callie wasn't sure whether to be relieved, flattered or angry. But before she could decide, Leoni climbed up on a chair and bawled for attention. When she had it, she got down and gestured for Jessie to join her. "As you know, our dear friend Jessie Baker is moving to California tomorrow. Of course we'll all miss her." Leoni paused to blow her nose and wipe at eyes suddenly filled with tears. "I'm going to have to keep this short, I seem to have caught a dad-blasted cold. But, as I was saying, we're going to miss you, Jessie. To keep us all in your heart, we pitched in to get you something special. Here." Leoni pulled a large package from behind a table and handed it to Aunt Jessie.

Aunt Jessie fumbled with the wrapping a moment, but then it finally fell away to reveal an oil painting of Sassafras Street in the height of summer. Flowers lined the sidewalk and rioted from hanging baskets. Summer tourists crowded the street and in the background, clearly marked, was Baker's with Aunt Jessie herself standing out in front. "Where did you ever get this?" she asked, her voice thick with tears.

"I had a photograph from a summer or two ago," Leoni explained. "I gave it to Julia Snodgrass down at The Corner Emporium, and she painted this picture of it."

"It's so lovely. Thank you, each one of you. I'll treasure it always." Aunt Jessie paused, close to tears. "I don't know what else to say."

"Then don't say anything," Leoni bellowed, "or you'll have us all bawling like babies. Come on everybody, eat up. I can't stand to see food go to waste."

Amidst the general hubbub, Callie saw Aunt Jessie slip away to her apartment, obviously in need of a few moments of privacy.

Maude was the first one through the buffet line and she seated herself next to Callie. "I saw you with Nick," she stated without preamble. "I've warned you about that, Caledonia."

The snarling pack of dogs came to mind again. "Look, Aunt Maude," Callie said, an edge of anger in her voice. "I understand your position and I've already told you I won't do anything to compromise Nick's job. But we work together. I can't avoid him all together."

"You mean *won't*," Maude sniped.

Callie had had it. "You're right," she flared. "I won't. I like him. We'll work better together if we're friends." It had taken a fit of anger to get her to see the truth, but she did like him...more than liked him. And that presented her with a new and completely different dilemma. One she preferred to think about without Maude surveying her through her shrewd black eyes.

"Humph," Maude snorted, but at least she omitted her usual harangue about the dire consequences that would follow any romantic entanglement. "Just remember, Caledonia, that I'll be back to check up on you two."

"Fine," Callie snapped. "It's your store. Now, if you'll excuse me, I'm going to mingle a little."

"Sit still, girl. I'm leaving. I need to talk to Nick."

Callie watched as her aunt moved through the crowd, parting it with all the stately majesty of a ship under full sail. "I've got to hand it to her," she muttered under her breath, "that woman has presence." It was just too bad she had to be such a dragon.

Maude found Nick and, while Callie still watched, talked earnestly to him for a few moments. Nick glanced in Callie's direction and caught her eye. Before he could look away, she saw a cold mask drop over his features. What in the world had Maude said to him to make him look like that?

She had cause to wonder the same thing again a few moments later when Nick came over to her. "I've made arrangements for someone else to get you home after the party," he said shortly. "I've got some things I need to do."

It was clear that Maude had something to do with his change in attitude. But what? "Fine," she said, trying not to let his chilly demeanor hurt.

"Don't be understanding with me," he snapped. "It won't work."

"What do you mean, it won't work?"

"I've got things I have to do and I won't feel guilty about it." He was really angry now.

"I'm not trying to make you feel guilty. If you can't take me home, you can't." Good Lord, he could be insufferable.

"It's not that I can't," he said, and then clamped his mouth shut.

"If you don't want to be with me, just say so."

"Not want to be with you?" He gave a bitter laugh. "You don't know the half of it, Caledonia." He rocked back on his heels. "I swear to God, I should quit this job."

She was furious now. "Then why don't you? It would certainly solve all of my problems," she said, regretting the words the instant they left her mouth.

She'd never seen anyone's expression grow quite as cold as his did at her hasty remark. "I told you once, Caledonia, that I have a job to do here and no one is going to prevent me from doing it. No one," he repeated.

"I assume you're referring to me."

"Assume the worst—" he began, but suddenly she'd had enough and cut him off in midsentence.

"I'm the one who should quit," she stormed. Everything she'd done for the past interminable week had been to protect him. And now here he was treating her as though she were nothing but a nuisance. She was too far past rational thought to remember he knew nothing of her pact with Aunt Maude.

To her surprise, he threw back his head and laughed. "That's rich," he hooted, and ran his hand through his hair, a sure sign he was exasperated.

"What do you mean?" she demanded.

"I mean, Callie, that the last thing on earth I want you to do is quit." His voice turned mocking. "After all, who's going to help me get the store remodeled?"

She stared at him for a long moment and then without another word, got up and hobbled away from him. She didn't have to wonder any longer how he felt about her. It was apparent the store came first, last and always in his affections. It was amazing how much the knowledge hurt. But what made her saddest of all was that Baker's suddenly meant so very little to her.

## Chapter Seven

Callie bid Aunt Jessie a tearful farewell the next day. "I'll miss you terribly," she said, her breath short, holding Jessie close.

Aunt Jessie was waging her own battle with tears. "Now, now, my dear, I'll see you very soon. I'll come back to visit as often as I can, and of course, you'll come to California."

"It won't be the same, Aunt Jessie."

"No, it won't. But maybe something wonderful will come along to take its place. Remember, 'When God closes a door, He opens a window.'"

"I hope He opens it in a hurry."

Aunt Jessie laughed. "There, you see, you're just like your Aunt Maude, even impatient with the Divine. Now, be a dear, dry your eyes and say goodbye to her."

Callie turned to Maude and hugged her quickly. "Goodbye, Aunt Maude. Take care."

Maude gave her one of her piercing black scowls. "You do the same."

Callie quickly moved away. Why did Maude's words always seem to carry some implied warning? There was really nothing more she could say to reassure her aunt she would follow her dictates about Nick. She had given her word and that would have to do. "Have you forgotten anything?" she asked Aunt Jessie.

"No, I don't think so. You take good care of Shadow for me and be sure to send her down as soon as the kittens all find a good home."

"I will, Aunt Jessie."

"And you'll write?" Aunt Jessie suddenly looked very old and vulnerable.

"Every day."

That brought a smile. "Every other day will do."

Maude shifted impatiently. "We're going to miss that plane, Jessie, if you don't hurry."

Aunt Jessie gave her sister one of her most serene looks. "Don't get your ulcers all in an uproar, Maude. We'll make it. Goodbye, Callie dearest." Aunt Jessie leaned close for one last hug. "Remember, follow your heart," she whispered, and then was gone.

Callie watched the two women disappear into a waiting cab and waved until it was out of sight around the corner. Then, with a deep sigh, she trudged back into the store.

Nick was waiting for her. "We'd better get to work."

"Of course," she said dully, far too dejected to do anything but agree with him.

"Snap out of it, Callie," he commanded. "I need you here one hundred percent."

That got to her. She'd just put Aunt Jessie into a cab so she could disappear to someplace in California and he wanted to get to work. So she hadn't been wrong about him. He really was an insensitive, unfeeling boor, and she told him so, too, at the top of her lungs, giving vent to all her pent-up emotions.

"Good," he said as her tirade wound to an end. "You're back. It's not like you to let a little setback get you down."

"You call losing the person I love most in this world a little setback?" she demanded.

"You've hardly lost her."

She whirled away from him. "I knew you wouldn't understand."

"Of course I understand, but as I see it, you have a choice to make here. You can either wallow in self-pity or hope for the best for both you and Aunt Jessie."

Of course he was right, but it infuriated her to admit it. "Give me a hammer," she said between clenched teeth.

He laughed. "Fortunately for the store's sake and my safety, we're past the hammer stage, at least for the time being. Today, we wallpaper."

In spite of everything, Callie felt a stirring of interest. "What do we do first?"

This time he hid his smile, turning instead to a makeshift table. "First we mix up the paste." He poured the contents of a white bag into a deep pan and added a generous portion of water. "You get to stir."

Callie took over at the pan while Nick cut a length of the yellow-print wallpaper she'd chosen. "You spread the paste on the paper and then hand it to me. I'll be on the ladder. I put it up and then we smooth out the wrinkles. Easy."

It did sound easy. Callie went through her routine and then handed the strip of paper to Nick, who hung it in place. Together they brushed it free of wrinkles and then started over again: cut, paste, hang, brush until half the day was gone and all of one wall was done.

"It looks wonderful," Callie decided, standing back for a better view.

"It does," Nick agreed, and climbed down from the ladder to stretch his cramped legs.

"Thanks," she said suddenly.

"For what?"

"For helping me over that rough spot."

"Then you're not mad anymore?"

"No." Not about that, anyway, she added silently.

"Good. Then you won't mind when I tell you I'm moving out of my hotel and into the upstairs apartment." He held up his hand to stop any objections. "After all, somebody has to look after Shadow and the kittens."

Actually, she was glad somebody was going to live up there. It was harder to think of it as empty than well taken care of. "I'll help you," she offered, and watched with amusement as his mouth dropped open in surprise.

"G-great," he finally managed to splutter. "How about this afternoon?"

It was his turn to compromise, she thought. "How about tomorrow? I'd like to get some more wall-papering done."

"Okay," he said after a short, internal struggle. "Tomorrow is good."

She sighed and stretched, feeling, if not happy, at least content. It was amazing what a little hard work could do for the soul. And the appetite. "I'm hungry," she said as her stomach rumbled. "Want to grab a bite to eat over at Leoni's before we start again?"

"We may get another chorus of 'Oh, Susanna,'" he warned.

"I'm starting to like that song."

Nick grabbed their coats off a nearby rack and helped Callie into hers. "Well, I'm not. It's been playing nonstop in my head since last night."

"There's only one way to exorcise it," she said firmly. "Think of another song. Something like 'Found a Peanut' or 'Ninety-nine Bottles of Beer on the Wall.'"

"Don't do this to me," he groaned as they headed out the door and across the street. "I'd rather have 'Oh, Susanna' stuck forever than either one of those."

"You pick a song then."

His eyes sought out hers. "How about 'Blue Moon'?"

Callie felt her heart turn over. She didn't think she ever wanted to hear that song again. It would only remind her of the foolish, romantic notions she'd entertained about Nick. The same ones he'd so thoroughly squashed the night before when he'd made it clear his career was more important to him than she was. I mean nothing to him, she told herself firmly, and he means nothing to me.

But if that were true, why couldn't she meet his gaze without her insides turning somersaults? "I—I like 'Oh, Susanna' just fine," she finally mumbled in reply, and hurried to keep a step ahead of him as they crossed the street.

Leoni greeted them at the door of the restaurant. "Callie," she boomed, "you poor lamb. You must be devastated." At least a dozen people paused in their eating to survey this example of total ruin.

To her surprise, Callie didn't even blush. Maybe she was getting used to Leoni's ways. "I'm fine, Leoni, really. Nick has been a big help."

"I'll just bet," Leoni hooted, and dug an elbow into Nick's ribs. "Atta boy," she said in a stage whisper guaranteed to carry to the farthest corner of the restaurant. "Maybe I ought to get the chef out here again." She stood dumbstruck while Nick howled with laughter, and even Callie couldn't resist a chuckle.

"Just a table, please," Nick finally gasped, wiping at his eyes.

Good-natured as always, Leoni accepted what was obviously a private joke and led them to *their* table overlooking Sassafras Street. "Enjoy, kids," she bellowed, and went in search of fresh prey.

Callie refused to meet Nick's gaze as they ate their lunch. She was afraid he might be able to read her pain and the reasons for it in her face.

"Callie?"

She kept her head down and sipped at her water, "Hmm?"

"Is there something wrong with my face today? Have I sprouted an extra nose or something?"

She cast him a brief glance. His face was as beautiful as always. "No."

"Then why won't you look at me?"

"No reason."

"Then do it."

She obeyed slowly. "Okay," she whispered, her heart in her eyes just as she knew it would be.

He reached over the table and took her hand in his. "Good. Now I want to tell you why I'm at Baker's."

"I thought Aunt Maude hired you."

"She did. I want to tell you a little more about why I took the job. I know I've mentioned my dad a couple of times," he went on. "He and I have been at loggerheads since the day I was born. As you've seen, I can be very stubborn and competitive."

Callie nodded. That was an understatement, to say the least.

"Well," Nick went on, "so can my dad. It was a problem when I was a kid, but when I went into the family business, it turned into a catastrophe. If he said it was Tuesday, I said it was Wednesday, whether it was or not. It got to the point where we couldn't be in the same room without fighting. You know, you can beat your head against a brick wall for only so long and then something's got to give, either your head or the wall.''

''What happened?'' she prompted when he paused.

''You asked me once if I ran away. I guess I did,'' he admitted, although it wasn't easy for him. ''But then I found out with a little distance from it all that I could choose to stop the conflict.''

''It was that easy?''

''Easy to leave the family business that was supposed to be mine one day?'' Nick grimaced. ''No, that was not easy. But now I see the conflict between us wasn't inevitable. When I chose not to fight anymore, the fight stopped.''

''So your dad won?''

He looked at her for a moment. ''That's the point,'' he said softly. ''There were no winners or losers. There were simply no players. My dad and I will never see eye to eye on very much, but some compromise on both our parts has brought us closer together. And that was worth everything, even the business.''

''So managing Baker's has been easier for you.''

''Easier?'' he asked, and gave a rueful laugh. ''You've got to be kidding. You Baker women are as stubborn and as quick-tempered as my father could ever hope to be. I think it must be my destiny to fight this battle over and over again until I finally get it right.''

"You make it sound like all of this is predestined or something."

"I don't mean to. Like I said before, everything is a choice. For example, if someone is interfering in your life, it's your choice to let them or not, for better or worse. It's as simple as that."

"What if the reason you let them interfere is right but the consequences are unbearable?"

He looked deeply into her eyes. "You hope for a day when you can explain why you're doing what you're doing."

If he only knew how close to home his words had come. She sighed suddenly and made him laugh again.

"You sound like the weight of the world is on your shoulders," he teased.

"Sometimes I feel like it is," she admitted.

"I could give you another lecture on how that's your choice, too, but I can see you're not ready for it. How about some fun instead?"

She pushed her plate aside. "What about the wallpaper?"

"It will still be waiting for us when we get back."

Her spirits began to lift. A little fun might be just what she needed to shake the blues away. "That sounds wonderful. What do you want to do?"

"Your choice."

"You haven't done much sightseeing, considering all the time you've spent up here. Maybe you'd like to see my favorite place."

"Inside or outside?"

"In Alaska?" she laughed. "Definitely outside."

"Let's go."

Within minutes they had piled into Callie's car. She headed south out of town along the gray sweep of water known as Turnagain Arm. "The mountains across the Arm," she explained, "are part of the Kenai chain."

Nick stared at the towering peaks and then let out a shout of surprise. "Callie, there's a bald eagle," he exclaimed, as eager as any boy.

She was glad that nature had decided to put on a show for him. It didn't always work out that way. "Sometimes, when the tide is out, you'll see several of them feeding along the tidal pools."

Nick watched the soaring eagle for a while and then shifted his gaze to her. "Where are we going?"

"You'll see. But first look over to the left. Sometimes Dall sheep will come right down the cliffs to the roadside."

Nick swiveled around and spent the next fifteen minutes scanning the craggy rocks that lined the highway. "Look," he finally cried, and pointed. Perched on a tall rock not fifteen feet off the roadway, a snow white sheep with long curved horns was placidly watching the traffic whiz by.

"Told you." Callie chortled, as proud of that sheep as if she'd put it there herself.

Nick seemed truly amazed. "What next, a polar bear?"

"Oh, that's right. You were disappointed when the bears didn't show up to meet you at the airport." She shook her head. "Sorry, but I can't produce one of those unless we go several hundred miles north of here. Or to the zoo," she added as an afterthought. "But if our luck holds, I think you'll like what we see next just as well."

She pulled the car into a turnoff and parked it. "Put your hat on," she instructed, "and your gloves. It's cold, especially with the wind coming in off the water."

"Do you think you should be out walking around on your foot?"

"It's better today, really. I've got the bandage on just to play on your sympathy."

He searched her face for an instant and then nodded his head. "At least part of that's the truth."

"I'm going to have to start wearing a mask," she said, only half in jest. "After all, a girl's got to have some secrets."

"Not from me," he protested, grinning.

"Especially from you," she retorted. She climbed from the car then and led him over an expanse of rocky ground to sit on a windswept promontory overlooking the restless gray waves.

"What are we looking for?" he finally asked after a few moments of scanning the empty inlet.

It was still early in the season yet, but with any luck, he'd see something to take his breath away. "There," she cried, grabbing his arm. "Look over there." She pointed to where something white and shining had rolled briefly from the waves.

Nick shook his head in disappointment. "I missed it."

"Don't worry, there will be another one, maybe even dozens."

"What is it, Callie? Tell me."

She pointed again. "Look. Do you see it?"

This time he did. A gleaming expanse of white lifted briefly from the water, turning as it dived again. He shook his head. "Is it some kind of fish?"

"It's a beluga whale, and there are sometimes hundreds of them in here. Now that you know what to look for, you'll see them surface, usually just one at a time, but sometimes several will come up at once in a sort of synchronized ballet."

They sat for a long while watching the whales. Not much passed between them except the camaraderie of a shared experience. At one point, Nick put his arm around her and pulled her close, but she thought it was as much for warmth as for any latent desire he felt for her.

At last he stirred and turned to her. "Your nose is all red," he commented.

"Thanks. So's yours."

"Why don't we go find a place that serves Irish coffee?"

"Sounds good to me."

Nick got up stiffly and helped her to stand. "I'm too old for this," he said, stomping his feet to restore the circulation.

"It does take someone quite young to sit and watch a bunch of whales swim by," she agreed, and then ducked away as he made a swipe at her hat. "Beat you back to the car," she called, already starting away at as fast a hobble as her still-bandaged foot would allow.

"That's not fair," he protested, but chased her anyway, catching her easily just short of the parking lot. "I've got you now," he said triumphantly.

She threw back her head and laughed up at him. "So what are you going to do with me?"

He sobered instantly. "This," he all but growled, and lowered his mouth to hers.

His lips were cold against hers, yet they somehow seemed made of fire. "Oh, Nick," she managed to say on a sigh, knowing she should pull away from him but unable to do so. And then she got lost, lost to his mouth, lost in his arms, and she wasn't sure she ever wanted to find her way back.

Forbidden fruit is always sweeter, she found herself thinking when at last Nick turned her loose and her sanity slowly returned. She should never have taken a bite of it, for now she knew she would hunger for more. "I think you should take me home," she told him.

But he seemed to have some regrets of his own. "I think I should, too," he said. "We'll do the coffee some other time."

"I'll just see myself in," Callie told him quickly when he pulled up in front of her apartment a silent hour later.

He agreed with a nod. "See you in the morning."

She paused and looked back at him. "Nick, I . . ." she began but then stopped. After all, what could she say to him? She knew she wasn't important to him in the broad scheme of things. He'd made that perfectly clear to her more than once. Oh, he'd enjoyed the few kisses they'd shared as much as she had. But his career came first. She would just have to accept that. She shrugged and turned away. "Never mind. I'll see you tomorrow."

They moved Nick's things into the upstairs apartment the next afternoon. They rearranged the furniture Aunt Jessie had left behind, supplementing the things Nick still needed with items from the store. Neither of them spoke of the day before, but they were polite to the point of stiffness, carefully stepping around each other as if some contagious disease had seized them both.

"I like it," Nick finally pronounced when the last lamp was plugged in.

"It's cozy," Callie agreed, and even though the apartment had been Aunt Jessie's for years, it had taken on a different feel with Nick's things scattered throughout. She sat down on a comfortable old sofa and immediately had a lap full of kittens. "Have you decided whether or not to keep one?" she asked as she stroked each tiny head in turn.

"At least one," Nick laughed. "The whole crew has kind of wormed its way into my heart."

"You can't keep six cats up here. Pretty soon there wouldn't be any room for you."

"It's going to be hard to pick."

"I like this one," she said, holding up a tiger-striped kitten. "He looks like a fighter."

"I still like the one with the four white paws." He chuckled. "Remember that first day when you told me Aunt Jessie was in the armoire? I thought for a minute I'd wandered into another dimension."

"Can you imagine how I felt when I had to tell you where she was?" They both laughed at the shared memory. "A lot has happened since then, hasn't it?"

His eyes caressed her face. "More than I ever expected."

She brushed the kittens from her lap and stood up, suddenly too agitated to remain still. "We have to make a pact to keep our relationship strictly professional," she said, pacing restlessly. "Make it and stick by it," she added.

"Is that what you want, Callie?"

"Yes, it is," she answered without hesitation. "I feel it's for the best." And it was. They couldn't go on stealing kisses when the consequences were so dire for both of them. He could lose his job and she could lose her heart.

"Can we be friends?"

"Of course," she said quickly and then added, "We already are."

"Are you sure this is *your* choice?"

She grew impatient with him. "Sometimes we do things because we aren't given any other choice."

He shrugged. "Sometimes it's hard to take the responsibility for our actions."

"I think you're being naive, Nick."

"Maybe. But then again, maybe you're the one who's being naive."

Her quick temper stirred to life. "This is all a bunch of esoteric nonsense. Life isn't as simple as you make it out to be."

"I never said life was simple."

"Don't try to placate me," she stormed.

"I'm not," he snapped, his own temper flaring.

"You make me so mad."

"You choose to be mad. I don't make you that way," he countered.

"I'm leaving."

"It's your choice."

She was beyond reason. "Why I ever thought I was in love with you I'll never know." And then she stopped, appalled at what had just come out of her mouth. She wasn't in love with him. She couldn't be. He was totally and completely impossible. She whirled and ran, clattering down the stairs, through the store and out the front door, leaving behind a very dazed Nick Logan.

Hard work must be the panacea for all ills, Callie decided as she brushed paste on what must have been the thousandth piece of wallpaper. It was hard to have emotions of any sort beyond weariness after three days of intensive, unaccustomed labor.

She hadn't wanted to come into work that morning, not after making such an outrageous statement to Nick the day before. She'd told him she loved him, and that just wasn't true. She still wasn't sure why she'd blurted it out to him. It must have been some sort of momentary mental aberration.

"I think that's enough paste, Callie," Nick said, breaking into her reverie.

She looked down and saw that she'd applied close to an inch-thick layer of paste to the strip of paper. "Sorry," she muttered, hurriedly scraping off the excess. "I guess I was daydreaming."

Nick leaned on one rung of the ladder, his eyes thoughtful as he looked down at her. "About what?"

"Oh, nothing. At least nothing important." She hoped he couldn't tell she was lying, but she wasn't about to repeat her gaffe from the night before and then have to postulate on why she'd made it. He'd probably say something about choices again.

"Do you want me to guess?" he went on in that lazy way of his.

"No," she said shortly, and all but hurled the strip of wallpaper up at him.

He deftly caught the dripping paper and with a grin still playing over his mouth, turned and applied it to the wall. "One more piece and that should do it," he told her.

"Good. I'll be happy when this is over."

He gave her another one of his significant looks. "The wallpapering?"

How was it possible for someone to make such an innocent question sound so full of insinuation? "Yes, the wallpapering," she retorted.

He chuckled, enjoying her obvious discomfort. "We'll nail up the wainscoting next, drop the ceiling, install light fixtures and lay the carpet."

"How much longer will it take?"

"Why?" His grin broadened. "Do you have... plans?"

He was starting to sound like Leoni, where every word carried some hidden meaning. But Callie wasn't going to rise to the bait. Look where it had gotten her yesterday. She shrugged as nonchalantly as she could. "I just want to know, that's all."

"It will take as long as it takes," was his cryptic reply.

"Great. Fine. It will take as long as it takes. I like that. It ranks right up there with all the choices I'm supposed to be making." She hadn't realized the depths of her frustration until she heard the sarcasm in her voice.

"This particular choice is mine," Nick said, and once more his eyes, softened to a misty blue, came to rest on her face.

"I would have thought you'd want to get the store reopened as quickly as possible."

"Profit is not my prime motive right now."

This was a departure, she thought, surprised. "What is, then?" She looked up and had that familiar sensation of falling into the azure pools of his eyes.

"Can't you guess?" he asked softly.

She shook her head, although for some strange reason her heart had begun its wild fluttering again.

He held her gaze for a moment longer and then gave a small nod, as if in answer to some unspoken question. "Think about it, Callie," he said, and reached down for the last piece of wallpaper.

## Chapter Eight

The wainscoting was relatively simple to put up, and except for a mashed finger or two from a miscalculated hammer blow, Callie enjoyed the change from wallpapering. Her relationship with Nick underwent another change, too. He treated her with unfailing kindness—his brand of friendship, she supposed. But he seemed to be waiting for something, and she wasn't sure what it was. She felt him staring at her while she worked, but when she confronted him with it, he denied it.

"You're letting your imagination run away with you," he said, and she felt like an idiot. But when she went back to work, she knew he was looking at her again, with eyes warm, intimate and very disturbing.

It made her pound her finger more often than usual, and at one point, she cried out in real pain.

Nick was instantly by her side, surveying the wounded finger. "Poor baby. Do you want me to kiss it?" He gave her an innocent smile that was belied by the impish glint in his eye.

She snatched her hand away and glared at him. "No, thank you."

"Pity," was all he said before he sauntered back to where he was working.

Callie felt as though she were under siege. His eyes, his knowing look, his smile, all seemed to beguile her. But what had started out as her resolve to keep him at arm's length for his own protection as well as hers, had somehow become a contest of wills instead. She had told him time and again she wanted nothing from him but his friendship. Why wouldn't he let it go at that instead of pushing her at every turn, asking for something she couldn't name and didn't want to give?

Callie was unaware of how her face gave the lie to her staunch denial. It was as if once spoken aloud, her words of love had taken root and flourished inside of her. And now, whenever her gaze would chance upon him, her eyes would melt and turn to the color of warm taffy. Her mouth would soften into an unconscious pout, begging for another kiss. Her expression would grow luminescent; and none of this she could hide.

In spite of it all, the store began to take shape. With the wainscoting installed, it was time to drop the ceiling. Nick, as usual, worked on the ladder while Callie played gofer down below. With every new ceiling tile laid in place, the old Baker's seemed to recede into the shadows. Callie liked the change but still found herself missing the old place.

Finally Nick noticed her growing sadness. "What's the matter?" he asked, looking down at her disconsolate face.

"I'm homesick," she admitted a little wistfully.

He didn't seem to need any explanation. "It's hard to let go," he agreed sympathetically. "I still miss my folks' store. Heck, I practically grew up there."

"Do you ever want to go back?"

"Back in time, sometimes. But go back physically after so much has happened? Never. It wouldn't be the same, anyway."

Callie nodded. "That's exactly how I feel. I miss what I can never have again."

"You need to find something to take its place, like I have here at Baker's."

Callie gazed up at him and thought just for a second that she had. But then she dismissed the idea as a silly flight of fancy born out of her homesickness. "That's what Aunt Jessie told me," she said instead. "At her going-away party."

"Your Aunt Jessie is a very wise woman."

Callie leaned against the wall, work forgotten. "I wonder how she is."

Nick glanced down at Callie. "I thought she called you a couple of days ago."

"Oh, she did," Callie acknowledged. "But Maude was standing right there. She could hardly tell me the truth."

"Did she sound unhappy?"

Callie thought a minute. "Really just the opposite," she confessed. "She seemed about as happy as the proverbial clam."

"Then maybe she is."

"How can she be?" Callie all but wailed.

"The question is, more aptly, do you want her to be?"

Nick had a talent for finding out where her Achilles' heel was. "It's the craziest thing," she said slowly as she formulated her thoughts into words, "but I want her to miss me as much as I miss her."

"And be miserable about it?" he asked, getting straight to the point.

Callie laughed. "I guess so. Like I said, crazy."

He gave her a tender look. "Not crazy. Very natural." He paused while he laid another ceiling tile in place and then took up the thread of their initial conversation again. "So," he asked, "what are you going to find to take the place of your old life?"

"Of course, I'll have my work here."

His face tightened, as if he were recalling something particularly unpleasant. "Have you ever thought of working somewhere else?"

"Why should I?" she countered. "Baker's has been my life for a long time. There's never been any reason to look for another job. Besides, I love it here." She laughed suddenly and tossed her head back to look up at him. "Why, are you planning to fire me?"

Nick's expression darkened. "I'd never do anything to make you leave."

She thought about Maude and found herself echoing his words. "I'd never do anything to make you leave, either." In fact, she would go to almost any lengths to protect him.

He turned away abruptly and picked up another tile. "Let's get back to work, then, before we're both fired for loafing on the job."

"Who's going to turn us in?" she pointed out with another laugh.

Abruptly, Nick set the tile down. "You're absolutely right," he exclaimed. "Who is going to turn us in?" He climbed down from the ladder, took her by the hand and pulled her toward the front door. "Come on, Callie," he said over her protests.

"But where are we going?" she asked, confused at his sudden change of attitude.

"We're going for a walk."

"But the store, the ceiling..."

"It'll be here when we get back."

"What's gotten in to you?" she asked, still resisting.

"Just an old saying I suddenly thought of. 'While the cat's away, the mice will play,'" he quoted, and then laughed. "The cat's a long way away today, and I think we should take advantage of the situation."

His mood was infectious. "Let me get the coats," she said, falling in with his small rebellion.

"That's the last practical thought you're allowed to have for the rest of the day," he admonished.

She agreed with a happy grin and ran for their coats.


And so their relationship changed yet again. Every day after that, they spent the morning working and the afternoon playing. They braved the cold and went to the zoo, had a picnic at a silent, slumbering park, sharing their food with a bold raven, and walked Anchorage's coastal bike trail.

Nick never once tried to take her in his arms again. Callie was both relieved, and if she had been truthful, disappointed. But she was having so much fun, it was easy to ignore her conflicting emotions.

One day, when their new routine was several weeks old, the weather changed and winter made its last retreat. A fierce wind blew in from the south, bearing the smell of the sea and warmer temperatures. As the very last of the snow began to melt, water dripped from the eaves and poured through down spouts in a restless torrent.

Nick laid his tools down for the day and sprawled on a nearby chair. "What do you want to do today? Go bowling?"

She shook her head emphatically. "Let's go for a walk."

"In this weather?"

"It's spring," she told him.

He shook his head. "No, it's not. Spring is fluffy white clouds, green grass, flowers—"

"Where you're from maybe," she broke in. "But spring in Alaska looks just like this. Lots of wind—"

It was his turn to interrupt. "Lots of mud."

"That, too," she agreed, laughing. "But I've got a pair of breakup boots that might fit you, so you don't have to worry about the mud."

"Breakup boots?"

"Alaskan tennis shoes." When he still looked puzzled, she relented and explained. "They're tall rubber boots we wear when the thaw—or breakup—sets in. If you were ever to watch the ice begin to move and flow on the rivers, you'd understand where the term comes from. The ice literally breaks up into great slabs. It's noisy, too. The ice groans and pops and then almost explodes as it starts to move."

"You'll have to show me sometime."

She looked up at him. "Really? Would you really like to see a river break up? You'd have to do some hiking to get into one."

He ran his hand through his hair in a gesture she found both familiar and endearing. "You sound pretty doubtful. Don't you think I can take it?"

"Let's see if you can take a short walk first," she retorted. It wasn't that she meant to sound skeptical, but he hadn't exactly had a lot of experience hiking through Alaska's back country wilderness.

"Is this a challenge, Miss Baker?"

She laughed. He was starting another round of his lighthearted banter. "It certainly is, Mr. Logan."

"What do I get if I pass your challenge?"

"What do you want?"

"Oh, Callie, what I could dream up with an opening like that! But ever the perfect gentleman, I'll merely demand a home-cooked dinner at your house."

That should have set alarm bells ringing in her head, but they were silent for once. "Who does the cooking?"

"You, naturally."

"Naturally," she said, her voice honey sweet. "And the cleanup?"

"You, of course."

"And if you should fail?"

"I won't."

She laughed again. "You have just a touch of self-confidence, don't you, Mr. Logan?"

"Just a touch," he acknowledged with a grin.

"But on the off chance you lose, then it's dinner at your place, agreed?"

"And I cook?"

"Naturally."

"Clean up?"

"But of course."

It was his turn to laugh. "You're on. What are you going to fix me?"

"First the walk, then we'll see who cooks whom what."

He looped his arm through hers. "Lead me to my boots."

Five minutes later they were slogging down Sassafras Street. Callie stopped so long to sniff delightedly at a newly budded daffodil, she had him stamping his feet.

"I'm freezing," he complained.

"Cold already? You poor flatlander." She shook her head sadly. "It looks like you're the one who's going to be cooking dinner tonight."

"Not a prayer. I can take it."

"Okay, tough guy, let's hike." She marched briskly to the end of Sassafras Street and led him down toward Cook Inlet. "We'll walk down into the Bootlegger's Cove area," she told him.

"It's colder by the water, isn't it?"

She smiled sweetly. "Would you prefer to stay here?" She could tell he did. For all the sunshine, it was cold out in the blustery wind.

He huddled deeper into his coat. "No, I love being the approximate temperature of an icicle. Lead on."

She almost relented then. But when he bent down and whispered in her ear, "How's your lasagna? I think that's what I want for dinner tonight," her resolve stiffened.

"My lasagna is famous," she said archly, "but at the rate you're going, you'll never taste it."

His laughter washed over her. "I'm pretty tenacious."

She remembered their bidding war at the antique auction and started making a mental shopping list. Just in case.

Bootlegger's Cove was full of quaint old houses and upscale offices. Callie and Nick wandered the streets, picking first one house and then another as their favorite until they ran out of streets and houses. "Let's go home," Callie finally said, conceding defeat. "I think you passed."

In high good humor, he picked her up and swung her around in a dizzying circle. "I told you I would," he whooped.

She looked into his laughing face and the world seemed to spin even faster. What a mixture of people he was, from the most serious to the most playful. And she delighted in every one. "We'll have to stop by a grocery store to get everything I'll need."

He set her on her feet but kept his arm firmly around her shoulders. "I want salad, too, and French bread. Cheesecake for dessert and, of course, a good bottle of wine."

"We won't eat until midnight if I have to make all of that," she protested.

He stopped and gave her a severe look. "You're not welshing on our bet are you?"

She shook her head and sent her hair flying. "I never go back on a bet. But I didn't realize you had seventeen courses picked out, either."

"Three courses, Callie. And I'll help. How's that for magnanimous?"

She wrinkled her nose at him. "You're a regular saint, Nicholas Logan."

He bent and whispered in her ear again, his breath warm and disturbing against her cheek. "We'll just see about that."

Callie knew it was time to make one of those choices Nick had talked about.

\* \* \*

The wonderful, spicy aroma of lasagna pervaded her tiny house. Callie sniffed appreciatively and then took another sip of the dry red wine Nick had picked out. This was turning out to be fun.

Nick wandered into the kitchen. "I love what you've done to your place," he said. "It looks just like you."

She smiled at him over the top of her wineglass, marveling at how he filled her house with his presence. "In what way?"

"The plants, all the antiques, pink-and-blue ruffles everywhere. Like I said, just like you." He moved to the back door and stared through the window. "What's out here?"

"Just backyard sorts of things, a shed, the deck...a hot tub," she finished with a mumble.

He looked over his shoulder at her. "A hot tub?" he asked casually. Too casually.

"Mmm," she answered, reading his mind. "But I rarely use it." That was a lie. She used it all the time. But she didn't think she wanted to climb into the wonderful hot water with the black velvet sky overhead and have him sitting just inches away. Who knew what would happen?

"Oh," was all he said, and to her relief, he dropped the subject. He turned back to her. "When do we eat? I'm starved."

"Right now. The salad is all ready and by the time we finish with that, the lasagna should be done."

They ate by candlelight in her small dining room. "To spring," he toasted, lifting his wineglass into the air.

"To spring," she murmured, and sipped the piquant wine again. "This is good," she told him.

"Have some more." He tipped the wine bottle over her glass, and she watched as the dark liquid splashed into it, catching and seeming to hold the candlelight in its ruby depths.

Conversation slowed as they ate the crisp green salad and crusty bread. They both agreed the fresh air had made them sleepy. But they revived over lasagna.

"This is terrific," Nick told her through a mouthful.

"I told you it was famous."

"Maybe you should go into the restaurant business."

She shook her head and her hair gleamed like fire in the dim light. "And leave Baker's? Not a chance. I love that store too much to ever leave."

He sobered suddenly. "Someday you might love a man that way."

She looked at him. "Maybe," she said, and wondered at the sudden leap of her heart.

"When you do, Caledonia, whoever he is, he'll be the luckiest man alive."

His eyes were blue velvet in the candlelight, his hair black satin, and just for an instant it was remarkably easy to imagine he was the one. But then, like leaves in a strong wind, her thoughts skittered away from the possibility. Not tonight, Caledonia, she told herself. Don't ruin this by thinking about what will never be.

She set her fork down suddenly. "I'm full," she announced, although she had hardly touched her lasagna.

"Let's have some entertainment before the cheesecake, then."

"Are you going to yo-yo again? Because I don't think my ceilings are high enough."

He tipped back in his chair, his gaze resting expectantly on her face. "I have something different in mind. Something you can participate in, too."

How neatly she fell into his trap. "Like what?"

"Let's get in the hot tub."

She should have objected immediately. Maybe it was the mellowing effects of the wine or the subtle inducement of the golden candlelight, but somehow she couldn't find the words to refuse and found herself nodding her acceptance.

Nick got up from his chair and walked around the table. He took her hand in his and drew her to her feet. "Why don't you bring your wineglass?" She nodded again and picked it up.

Callie felt something building inside of her, some dark yearning that swept her up and carried her past any ability to stop whatever might happen next. She saw with unusual clarity that every event of the past few weeks had propelled her to this moment.

Together, without saying a word, they walked out to the hot tub. Wraiths of steam arose off its surface and curled into the night. "Do you want to get in first?" he asked her.

Callie nodded. "Turn around," she said, and when he did, she quickly set about removing her clothes. "Don't look," she ordered.

Pale in the moonlight, Callie paused at the edge of the hot tub and out of long habit, tested the water. It was then when she was preoccupied that Nick cast a long look over his shoulder. He caught his breath at her beauty, and a silent shudder passed over his body.

Callie climbed into the tub and sank into the steaming water. "Your turn," she called.

Nick turned around slowly. "Callie," he began.

"Yes, Nick?" Her eyes were dark pools in the moonlight.

Again that shudder passed over him. "Never mind," he said gruffly. "Close your eyes."

Her eyelids fluttered shut. But unable to stop herself, she peeked at him through the long sweep of her lashes. The moonlight sculpted his body into silver planes and ebony hollows, hiding much, but revealing enough to fire her imagination. She burned and shook, alternately touched by flames and ice, finally closing her eyes completely to block out the sight of him.

She heard the water splash and felt his presence next to her. "You can open your eyes now," his voice rumbled in the darkness.

Her eyes opened slowly, taking in first the lapping water in front of her and then the dark trees ahead, silhouetted against the still darker sky. "This feels good," she murmured, keeping her eyes on the moonlit sky.

He sighed and leaned back against the edge of the redwood tub. "It does, doesn't it?"

Callie chanced a quick look at him. In all her life she had never seen such a beautiful man. She shivered again and sank deeper into the bubbling water.

"Callie, tell me the truth. Don't you ever really use this?"

She laughed at herself and then confessed, "I come out here all the time."

"Then why did you say you didn't?"

She found her eyes on him again and couldn't look away. What could she say to him beyond the obvious truth? "Nick, I . . . that is," she fumbled, "we don't have any clothes on."

She could hear his smile. "That's true," he replied. "Does the situation offend your modesty?"

Her modesty? No, it wasn't that. It was that she . . . wanted him so much. And then she knew. She wanted him because she loved him. She hadn't made some stupid slip of the tongue when she'd told him that so many days before. She'd loved him then just like she loved him now. Had loved him, she realized with dawning wonder, from the moment she'd battled him at the auction.

"Callie?"

She had no idea how much time had elapsed between his question and her incredible discovery. A minute, an hour, a lifetime? "Nick, I need to tell you something."

He reached across the space separating them and lifted a strand of her wet hair. "Did I ever tell you, Callie, that you have the most glorious hair?" he said musingly, as if he hadn't heard her. "I spend half my time with you wondering what color it really is, whether it's red or chestnut or something in between. And I spend the other half, trying to keep my hands away from it. It's silk, Callie. Beautiful, soft silk."

He lifted another strand and then another until he had a handful. "Come here," he said, his voice husky. He gently tugged her toward him until her lips hovered just inches from his. "Callie, this is no stolen kiss. I've planned and plotted it for weeks now." He lowered his mouth even closer to hers. "Ah, Callie," he sighed. "I'm bewitched." He kissed her then, his lips tender, heartbreakingly gentle.

It was Callie who deepened the kiss. With a soft moan, she beckoned his probing tongue into her mouth. Then she wrapped her arms around his neck and pressed closer to him until there was nothing between them except the barest sheen of warm, lapping water.

Nick's mouth left hers and trailed down the sweep of her long neck. When he found the throbbing pulse at its base, he paused and pressed a light kiss there. And then his lips continued their downward journey through the shadowed valley between her swelling breasts.

Callie threw her head back and shuddered with wave after wave of desire. Through half-closed eyes, she saw the moon sailing through the star-silvered night and almost wept with an emotion as deep and as wide as the night sky.

But then, as Nick's mouth brushed over her breasts, she was lost to thought, to reason, to everything except him.

"Callie," he whispered long minutes later.

"Yes, Nick?" she answered in a voice grown dark and ragged with need.

"The phone's ringing."

"Let it."

"It's been ringing for almost five minutes now."

A shred of concern crept into her mind. Maybe it was an emergency of some kind. After all, it was very late for any casual phone call. And then an even worse thought emerged. Maybe something had happened to Aunt Jessie. "I should answer it. Close your eyes while I get out."

He laughed. "Not a chance."

With a small laugh, she splashed water in his eyes and while he yelled and spluttered with surprise, she leaped from the tub and snatched up her clothes on her way to grab the phone. "Hello," she said breathlessly, aware she was dripping all over the floor.

"Caledonia, where have you been? I've been calling for—"

"Aunt Maude," she broke in, "is it Aunt Jessie? Has something happened?"

Even from three thousand miles away Aunt Maude's characteristic snort of impatience came through loud and clear. "There's nothing wrong with Jessie. Why should there be? I've been trying to get a hold of you for days now, but no one ever seems to be at the store. I finally decided to try at this unholy hour. Just what is going on up there, young lady?''

Callie's eyes strayed to the back porch where Nick's face was still a pale blur in the hot tub. ''Nothing,'' she lied over a leap of desire.

''Nothing to the store, you mean.''

Callie stepped away from her view of the porch and tugged on her clothes. ''That's not true, Aunt Maude. The store is coming along beautifully. You should see it.''

''I intend to. I'll be there one week from today, and it had better be finished or heads will roll.''

Callie gulped. Could they possibly get the store done in that short amount of time? ''We'll look forward to seeing you.''

''Where's Nick,'' her aunt asked abruptly.

''Are you having trouble finding him, too?'' It seemed a safe enough reply.

''Humph,'' Maude retorted. ''If I didn't know better I'd say he was there with you. But that would be foolhardy, now wouldn't it?''

''It certainly would,'' Callie agreed, and then heard Nick enter the room. She turned and saw that he had pulled on his jeans but left his chest bare. It was lightly furred with damp curly hair that veed down over his flat belly and disappeared past his waistband. She caught her breath, remembering how she had been pressed so intimately against him only moments before.

"Caledonia?" Maude said sharply in her ear, "are you still there?"

"Yes, Aunt Maude," she said, although her voice seemed to come from very far away. "I'm still here."

"Do you have a message for Jessie?"

Callie smiled. "Tell her I'm about to take her advice."

"What advice is that?"

"She'll know."

Maude snorted again. "Very well. I'll see you in one week."

"One week," Callie echoed, and hung up the phone.

"Maude?" Nick asked.

"Maude," she answered. "She expects the store to be finished in one week or, to quote her, 'heads will roll.' Do you think we can do it?"

"We'll have to work around the clock," he said, his voice full of doubt.

"That's fine with me."

"There won't be any time to play," he reminded her.

Callie nodded, smiling serenely. "I know."

He looked disappointed. "You mean you don't mind?"

"No, I don't." A plan was forming in her mind, a wonderful plan she should have thought of long before this. But she hadn't realized how much she loved Nick before this. She moved close to him and with one finger gently traced the outline of his mouth. "Will you come to dinner again, one week and one day from tonight?'' There was no mistaking the promise in her voice.

He caught her around the waist. "What are you up to, Callie?"

"You'll find out in a week and a day." She broke free of him and leaned against a nearby table. "But until then, I think we need to agree to stick strictly to the business at hand."

"We've made that agreement before," he pointed out with a knowing grin.

"But this time we have to promise to do it."

He searched her face. "Okay," he finally agreed. "But just for eight days. And then I come after you, whether you're ready for me or not."

She could only nod her assent as desire once more licked at her body.

# Chapter Nine

Callie knew she had never worked so hard in her entire life. Their days started before breakfast and went on until long past dinner. And with only two days left until Maude's expected arrival, there were still a million things to do. The wall lighting had to be installed, the carpet laid, the trim nailed up and, of course, the store put back into order.

She never asked Nick if they were going to make it, but by the grim look that had settled around his mouth, she knew their chances weren't very good. We'll do it, she told herself a dozen times every day, but as yet hadn't been able to convince herself of it.

Their tempers had run as short as their time. Callie didn't want to be irritable but she was so tired she couldn't seem to help it. And Nick had turned into a veritable beast, snarling and growling at the least provocation until she didn't know whether to hit him or hug him.

But one thing remained constant, her love for him. Having at last admitted it, she was free to plum its depths. I love him, she whispered as she hammered. I love him, she sang when he left the store for a few minutes. She would tell him so, too, as soon as the store was finished and she had dealt with Aunt Maude.

"Callie," Nick called to her now, "come hold this light fixture in place while I mark where it should go."

Obligingly, she left off what she was doing and trotted over to him. "I've got it," she said, steadying the heavy Art-Nouveau-style fixture against the wall.

"Are you sure?"

"Sure," she answered, and he pulled his hands away. But the fixture was heavier than she'd expected and it slipped from her grasp. It fell to the floor and shattered, sending shards of glass flying everywhere.

"Dammit!" Nick exploded. "I thought you said you had it."

"Hey," she snapped, "you could have warned me how heavy it was."

"Don't blame this on me. You're the one who dropped it."

Her temper skyrocketed. "You should have known it would be too heavy for me."

Nick lowered his face to hers and glared into her eyes. "I didn't know you were such a wimp."

They were a scant inch apart now. "Wimp?" she cried, her voice rising a full octave. "In case it escaped your notice, I'm a woman. I'm not supposed to have huge bulging biceps like you, you...you big ox.''

Still nose to nose with her, his face creased into a sudden grin. ''How would the wimp like a kiss from the ox? I mean, we're this close and I hate to waste the opportunity.''

She couldn't have said no to him even if she'd wanted to. ''Okay,'' she sighed, ''just one.''

''I think we played this game once before,'' he said, eyes full of remembered mischief. ''But I agree, just one kiss.'' He put his arms around her and kissed her then with all the pent-up longing four days of forced abstinence could bring.

Callie poured her heart into that kiss, telling him with her lips everything she felt, every hope she had. She clung to him and willed the kiss to go on and on, to never stop, to keep the world at bay. And for long moments it did just that. But the human body requires oxygen, and at last Callie had to pull away.

''That was some kiss,'' Nick managed to tease, his voice still rough with passion.

Callie could only nod.

''Do you think we should try just one more?''

That made her laugh. ''One more and I'll faint.''

''One more,'' he echoed, ''and this store won't ever get done.''

Callie looked down at the floor. ''What are we going to do about the light?''

''Why don't you run to the store and see if they have another one while I clean up this mess.''

''What if they don't?''

He grinned. "Then we punt."

Fortunately the lighting store did have another one and disaster was averted. By nightfall all the fixtures were safely installed and they quit for the day. "The carpet layers are scheduled in tomorrow," Nick told her.

"We're not going to do it?"

"That's way beyond my expertise," he admitted. "And besides, we could use the help."

"What will we do?"

"There's not much we can do until the carpet's down."

"There must be something," she insisted.

"We could soak our troubles away in the hot tub."

Callie looked up into his eyes and very nearly gave in. But no, she had some unfinished business to take care of before she could allow herself that luxury. "Why don't we decide where we're going to put everything. That way, we'll have a jump on the game when we start moving things back into place."

"I like my idea better."

She touched him lightly on the cheek. "I'd rather face Aunt Maude with all my ducks in a row," she explained, and he nodded his understanding.

"I'll walk you home," he said. "We both need plenty of sleep tonight. I have a feeling we're in for two very long days."

Although the night was brisk, spring was still very much in the air as they strolled outside. "When does summer start?" he asked suddenly.

"The trees will green up soon, around mid to late May."

"Does it get any warmer?"

She had to laugh. "Much," she assured him. "Into the sixties and even seventies on a really hot day."

"You call the seventies hot?"

"When you're used to cool weather..."

"Cold weather," he amended.

"Okay, cold weather, the seventies can seem pretty warm. And don't forget we have almost twenty hours of daylight in the summer."

He looked up into the dark sky. "I can't even imagine that."

She tucked her arm through his. "Just wait. Alaska in the summer is the most beautiful spot on earth."

He looked down at her. "I find it pretty beautiful right now."

She wanted to snuggle closer but decided to resist. Just two more days, she told herself firmly, and then things will be different.

At her front door, Nick kissed her chastely on the forehead. "Sweet dreams, Callie," he murmured.

It was all she could do to keep from throwing herself at him. "Good night, Nick. See you in the morning," she replied, and watched until he'd disappeared back up Sassafras Street.

Once in bed, Callie rehearsed her impending confrontation with Maude. For she had little doubt a confrontation was imminent. She'd decided on a course of action that would protect Nick's job *and* leave her free to pursue a relationship with him. What she had in mind wasn't going to be easy, but it would be worth it.

The store was finished. The last nail had been pounded, the last bit of spilled paint cleaned up, the last light fixture hung in place. And now it waited as a debutante might, cloaked in its new finery, ready for its entrance into society.

Callie stood in the middle of the store and looked around her with awe. She and Nick had spent several hours polishing most of the antique furniture so that everywhere she looked, she saw the rich gleam of beeswax. Pots of trailing English ivy and red geraniums bloomed from every conceivable nook and cranny. The carpet was a velvety expanse of gray, the wainscoting a warm lemony yellow that was repeated in the wallpaper. The cut-glass chandeliers and wall sconces added just the right touch of elegance to the overall decor. The store was everything she'd envisioned it would be, and more, going well beyond her wildest expectations.

Nick stood only a few feet away from her taking his own inventory. "Wow," he finally muttered.

"It's better than wow, it's fantastic, incredible, gorgeous."

He laughed. "Like I said, wow!"

"Maude should be here any minute."

"Nervous?"

"No," Callie lied.

"Me, neither," he said so solemnly, she knew he was lying, too.

"I wish I had time to go home and change. I look like Cinderella before her fairy godmother arrived." Callie looked down at her ragged jeans and dusty sweater and grimaced.

"Maude will be so overawed by all of this, she won't notice anything else," Nick assured her.

Callie saw a yellow cab pull up in front of the store. "It's time to find out," she said, and pointed.

They both watched as Maude, clothes perfect, hair indomitably styled even after several hours of traveling, emerged from the back of the cab. She marched toward them, and they had only time for a shared glance before she burst into the store.

"Nick," Maude said briskly, setting her suitcase down. "Caledonia. You're rather disheveled today."

Callie bit back a laugh and chanced a peek at Nick. He, too, seemed to be having trouble keeping a straight face. "Welcome to the new Baker's," she said, recovering her composure. "Isn't it beautiful?"

"Humph," Maude snorted, her sharp eyes darting quickly through the store. "Give me a tour," she commanded, "so I can judge for myself."

Nick, with Callie beside him, conducted Maude through the store, keeping up a running commentary as they walked. "As you can see, the color scheme is both contemporary yet warm. We feel it is a perfect foil for the antiques."

Callie smiled, remembering the fight they'd had over that. Only the first of many and yet look what they had accomplished with give and take, compromise, hard work and a lot of love.

"I don't like the lights," Maude complained. "They're too fancy."

"We felt anything more functional would detract from the atmosphere we were trying to achieve," Nick said smoothly, and Callie wondered if he regretted giving in on the track lighting. But then he gave her an almost imperceptible wink, and she knew he didn't.

They made it back to the rear of the store and Maude settled herself regally at the old rolltop desk. "I'd like a cup of tea," she announced imperiously.

Nick and Callie were ready for this. "I'll just go upstairs and get it," he said as prearranged. Callie had already told him she needed a few minutes alone with her aunt.

As soon as Nick had disappeared, Callie squared her shoulders and turned to Maude. But her aunt beat her to the punch.

"So, Caledonia, did you keep up your end of the bargain or am I going to have to fire that young man?"

Callie's eyes blazed. "Are you unhappy with what we've done to the store?"

"No," Maude answered grudgingly. "It's really quite attractive. But you didn't answer my question."

"Let me answer it this way. I love this store as if it were my very own. I've put my heart and soul into it for years now. With that in mind—" Callie hesitated, took a deep breath and forged on "—I quit."

Maude's mouth dropped open. "You what?"

"I quit." The second time she said it was much easier. "No one has the right to decide who I associate with."

"Does this mean you've formed some sort of attachment for that young man?" Maude demanded.

"I don't have to answer that. But I will anyway. Yes, I've formed an attachment for him. I love him." She said it again for the sheer joy of hearing it out loud. "I love him, Aunt Maude. I'm quitting so that you won't have to fire him."

Suddenly the enormity of what she'd just done swept over her. She didn't regret her action, but she would have been inhuman not to feel some grief. Tears stung her eyes, and rather than let her aunt see them, she turned and ran. "Tell Nick I'll be back," she managed to say over her shoulder and then she fled outside into the cool evening air.

She was half a block away before she realized she'd left her coat behind. But she wasn't ready to go back just yet. Leoni's place, lit up with cheerful pink-and-green neon, beckoned to her through the gathering twilight, and she headed in that direction. Maybe a cup of coffee would help.

Leoni swept over to her just as Callie seated herself at the counter. "What is it, Callie?" she boomed. "You break up with that fellow of yours."

Callie shook her head, smiling in spite of herself. "Just the opposite, Leoni."

Eyes avid, Leoni slid onto the stool next to her. "Did he ask you to marry him?"

Since her voice had carried throughout the diner, Callie decided to announce her intentions to the crowd. "I'm going to ask him."

"No!" Leoni exclaimed, surprised into near silence.

"Yes," Callie assured her. "I love him and I think he loves me."

The door opened and Nick appeared, his face thunderous. "Callie, what have you done?"

Heads swiveled from Callie to Nick and back to Callie again. "I quit," she said calmly.

"You can't. I just quit."

The unfolding drama held everyone in their seats.

"Why in the world would you go and do something as stupid as that?" Callie demanded.

"So you won't have to leave."

"But I already have. Maude said that if you and I fell in love, she'd fire you. After all she can't fire me, I'm family."

"She told me that if we fell in love, she'd fire you. After all, she has a contract with me."

Callie blanched, recalling all her foolish suspicions about him. "We've been had."

"Royally."

Leoni nudged her in the side. "Ask him about the love part," she whispered, loud enough so that even the cook poked his head out of the kitchen to hear the answer.

"So why did you quit?" Callie asked again.

"Why did you?"

"I asked first."

Nick ran his hand through his hair. "Did anyone ever tell you, Caledonia Baker, that you are the most exasperating woman?"

"You have, several times," she said calmly. "Now, quit stalling and answer the question. Why did you quit Baker's?"

He ran his hand through his hair again. "Because," he finally roared, "I love you, Callie, and I didn't want you to have to choose between Baker's and me."

"But I already have. I love you, Nick Logan, more than any store. I knew if I quit, you wouldn't have to choose between Baker's and me."

Leoni elbowed her again. "Ask him the next part."

Callie faltered for an instant. But then Aunt Jessie's words came back to her. *Just follow your heart, dear,* and that's what she intended to do, regardless of the outcome. She looked around for a moment, suddenly aware of their rapt audience. "Come with me," she told Nick, and grabbing him by the hand tugged him into the kitchen. Leoni and half her patrons crowded to the door behind them, pushing and shoving for the best position even as they were shut out.

The chef looked up from the large pot he was stirring on the stove. "You need something?"

"Some privacy?"

He glanced from Callie to Nick and back again. "Okay, lady, you've got two minutes and then I've got to get back in here and stir my soup." As he brushed by them on his way out, he clapped Nick heartily on the shoulder. "Good luck, my friend," he murmured in an aside. "I think you're going to need it with this one."

Callie had to wait for Nick to quit laughing before she could ask him her all-important question. "I love you, Nick," she said again after taking a deep steadying breath, "and I think we should get married."

He didn't pause, not even for a heartbeat. "I accept," he said, and gathered her into his arms and kissed her soundly on the mouth.

"Callie!" Leoni shouted through the closed door. "Callie Baker, you come out of my kitchen right now and tell me what he said."

Nick lifted his head and laughed. "I think you better do what she says. No telling what might happen next."

"It's bound to be horrible," Callie agreed, grinning, and arm in arm they walked back into the restaurant.

Leoni took one look at Callie's flushed and smiling face and began to clap. "We're going to have a wedding, folks." But before the crowd could so much as stir, the door to the street opened behind them and Maude stepped into the restaurant. "The villain of the piece," Leoni announced in a loud aside for the edification of her guests, and they nodded in fascinated unison.

Maude, oblivious to Leoni, trained her eyes on Nick and Callie. "Caledonia," she rasped, "I see you and your young man have come to some sort of an understanding."

Callie broke free of Nick's embrace and faced her aunt. "Yes, we have." She smiled up at him. "We're getting married."

"Since you've both quit, it seems as if I'm going to have to make different arrangements for the store."

Callie nodded. "Yes, you are." She hated to see strangers working in her beloved store. But she had found something so much more important.

"Perhaps you and Nicholas would like to come back over to Baker's and hear what I have in mind."

Leoni's patrons moaned their disappointment. "Oh, just spill it, Maude," Leoni said impatiently. "You can't leave us hanging."

Maude seemed to focus for the first time on their sizable audience. "Fiddlesticks! I can do anything I darned well please." And then her face softened. "But what the heck, I don't have anything to hide." She leveled her black, glittering gaze on Callie and Nick. "I don't have any use for an untended antique store, especially one three thousand miles from my home. It's yours, if you want it. Consider it a wedding gift."

Callie was dumbstruck. Maude was giving them Baker's for a wedding gift? Impossible.

Nick, too, seemed to be having his doubts. "Could you repeat that?"

"What's the matter, boy, are you going deaf? I said I'm giving you Baker's, and good riddance, too. It will probably land you in the poorhouse."

Callie threw her arms around Nick and hugged him tight. And then, with tears glistening in her eyes, she turned to Maude. "I'm going to hug you, too," she warned, and wrapped her aunt in a warm embrace. "Thank you," she murmured. "You old softy."

Maude harumphed and spluttered and then smiled slyly. "Everything worked out pretty well, didn't it, girl?"

Callie stared into her aunt's face. "Why, you planned all this, didn't you?"

Maude wouldn't answer, but her eyes seemed to twinkle slightly. "We all got what we wanted, didn't we?"

Callie could only nod. It was true. Jessie got companionship her own age; Maude her sister's unquestioning love. Callie got Nick and he got her, and together they got Baker's. Even Machiavelli couldn't have done a neater job of arranging their lives. She started to laugh and couldn't stop even as tears filled her eyes and coursed down her cheeks.

"Nick, close your eyes."

"Not a prayer."

"Then I won't get into the hot tub."

Nick scrutinized her stubbornly set face and relented with a sigh, closing his eyes. "Okay, Callie, you win. But hurry up, it's cold out here."

Callie dropped the beach towel she'd wound around her body and as was her custom, quickly tested the water before sliding in. In that moment, Nick opened his eyes and frankly perused her shapely backside. Oblivious to his stare, she stepped into the water and sank into its bubbling depths. "Your turn," she called.

"You know the drill," he said to her.

"You want me to close my eyes now, right?"

"Right."

She squeezed her eyes shut and when she thought it was safe, opened them a crack. He was so beautiful standing there in the black velvet night, she caught her breath.

"Caledonia!" he roared, "You're peeking."

"Am not," she denied, unable to suppress a telltale grin.

"Are, too," he said, and stepped into the tub, causing the water to lap higher around her breasts.

"Can I open them now?" she asked, her voice pure honey.

"They are open, you little minx."

"No, really, Nick, I've still got them closed."

He sat down beside her, so close his thigh brushed against hers in a disturbingly intimate way. "Callie," he whispered into her ear, his breath stirring a tendril of her hair, "when are you going to learn I can tell you're lying just by looking at your face?"

Her eyes popped open. "You cannot."

"Can, too. I knew that you loved me from the first day we met."

"How could you, when I didn't even know it myself?"

"It's all in your eyes, Callie, so don't ever try to hide anything from me."

She sighed and leaned against his shoulder. "Wasn't it a lovely day?" she said, changing the subject.

"Wonderful," he agreed.

"I love my necklace." Her hand strayed to the Edwardian pendant nestled between her breasts.

"I bought it just for you."

She laughed. "Now who's the liar? You bought it because you can't bear to lose."

"Didn't I tell you that I loved you from the first day we met?"

"Oh, Nick," she sighed, "did you really?"

"I can tell you the exact moment. When you turned to me and told me how stupid I'd been to up the bid."

"You loved me then? I wasn't very nice."

"No," he agreed, and then, after she'd splashed him, paused and wiped the water from his eyes. "But I knew you had all the qualities I was looking for in a woman," he finally went on.

"Like what?"

"Shrewish tongue, vile temper—" He neatly caught her hand to prevent another soaking and brought it to his lips, kissing each one of her fingertips in turn. "The biggest brown eyes I'd ever seen," he said between kisses, "and a mouth no man could resist."

Callie settled against his side again, and he put his arm around her. "Aunt Jessie looks good," he observed.

"She does, doesn't she?"

"How did she ever get your dress made in time?"

Callie thought of the beautiful white confection she'd worn that afternoon and smiled. "She and Aunt Maude both worked on it around the clock."

"That must have been something to see—and hear." They laughed together.

Callie snuggled closer. "Leoni outdid herself with the food."

Nick nodded even as his hand slid down her arm. "She almost got me to agree to 'Oh, Susanna' for the wedding march."

Callie twisted to look up into his face. "No!"

Nick laughed and bent closer. "Would you have refused to walk down the aisle if I had?"

She caught her breath as his hand slid even lower. "No," she whispered.

"That's good. Because even if you had, Mrs. Logan, I would have carried you down myself. Remember, we had a date in the hot tub I wasn't about to let you postpone again."

"You only had to wait an extra ten days."

"Ten days too long," he growled, and then his lips met hers and conversation was at an end.

"Nick," she murmured much later.

"Hmm?" His voice was drowsy.

"It's snowing."

Nick opened his eyes a crack and saw that large, lacy snowflakes were drifting out of the night sky. "I thought you said it was spring."

"It is."

"But it's snowing. It's not supposed to do that in the spring."

She shook her head sadly. "It looks like I've got a lot to teach you about living up here."

Nick pulled her close and feathered a kiss on her lips. "Why don't you give me my first lesson."

"Which one is that?" she said with a sigh, twining her arms around his neck.

"The one that begins like this—" he kissed her again "—and ends..." But his words trailed away leaving only the silence of the night and the beautiful, drifting snow.

* * * * *

# Silhouette Romance®

## COMING NEXT MONTH

**#724 CIMARRON KNIGHT—Pepper Adams**
*A Diamond Jubilee Book!*
Single mom Noelle Chandler thought she didn't need a knight in shining armor. Then sexy rancher Brody Sawyer rode into her life. This is Book #1 of the *Cimarron Stories*.

**#725 FEARLESS FATHER—Terry Essig**
Absent-minded Jay Gand fearlessly tackled a temporary job of parenting. After all, how hard could it be? Then he found out, and without neighbor Catherine Escabito he would never have survived!

**#726 FAITH, HOPE AND LOVE—Geeta Kingsley**
Luke Summers's ardent pursuit of romance-shy Rachel Carstairs was met by cool indifference. But Luke was determined to fill the lovely loner's heart with faith, hope...and his love.

**#727 A SEASON FOR HOMECOMING—Laurie Paige**
**Book I of HOMEWARD BOUND DUO**
Their ill-fated love had sent Lainie Alder away from Devlin Garrick— and her home—years ago. Now, Dev needed her back. Would her homecoming fulfill broken promises of the past?

**#728 FAMILY MAN—Arlene James**
Weston Caudell's love for his estranged nephew warmed wary Joy Morrow, but would the handsome businessman leave as quickly as he'd come—with her beloved charge...and her heart?

**#729 THE SEDUCTION OF ANNA—Brittany Young**
Dynamic country doctor Esteban Alvarado set his sights on Anna Bennett, but her well-ordered life required she resist him. Yet Anna hadn't counted on Esteban's slow, sweet seduction....

## AVAILABLE THIS MONTH:

 *Silhouette Romance* ®

# DIAMOND JUBILEE CELEBRATION!

It's the Silhouette Books tenth anniversary, and what better way to celebrate than to toast *you*, our readers, for making it all possible. Each month in 1990 we'll present you with a DIAMOND JUBILEE Silhouette Romance written by an all-time favorite author! Saying thanks has never been so romantic...

The merry month of May will bring you SECOND TIME LUCKY by Victoria Glenn. And in June, the first volume of Pepper Adams's exciting trilogy Cimarron Stories will be available—CIMARRON KNIGHT. July sizzles with BORROWED BABY by Marie Ferrarella. Suzanne Carey, Lucy Gordon, Annette Broadrick and many more have special gifts of love waiting for you with their DIAMOND JUBILEE Romances.

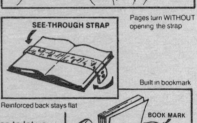

# *Silhouette Romance*®

## CIMARRON STORIES

### A TRILOGY BY PEPPER ADAMS

Pepper Adams is back and spicier than ever with three tender, heartwarming tales, set on the plains of Oklahoma.

#### CIMARRON KNIGHT...coming in June

Rugged rancher and dyed-in-the-wool bachelor Brody Sawyer meets his match in determined Noelle Chandler and her adorable twin boys!

#### CIMARRON GLORY...coming in August

With a stubborn streak as strong as her foster brother Brody's, Glory Roberts has her heart set on lassoing handsome loner Ross Forbes...and uncovering his mysterious past....

#### CIMARRON REBEL...coming in October

Brody's brother Riley is a handsome rebel with a cause! And he doesn't mind getting roped into marrying Darcy Durant—in name only—to gain custody of two heartbroken kids.

**Don't miss CIMARRON KNIGHT, CIMARRON GLORY and CIMARRON REBEL—three special stories that'll win your heart...coming soon from Silhouette Romance!**

CIM-1

**Silhouette Books proudly
announces the arrival of**

*Birds Bees
and Babies*

**JENNIFER GREENE
KAREN KEAST
EMILIE RICHARDS**

Available now for the first time, Silhouette Books
presents a loving collection of three stories
celebrating the joys of motherhood.

BIRDS, BEES AND BABIES is a gift from the
heart by three of your favorite authors. Jennifer
Greene, Karen Keast and Emilie Richards have
each created a unique and heartwarming romance
devoted specially to the love between man, woman
and child.

It's a lullaby of love . . . dedicated to the romance
of motherhood.